Noah's Fire

Noah's Fire

Lynn Howard

Published by Twisted Heart Press, LLC

Chapter One

Hollyn's feet hit the ground hard, pinecones and twigs digging into her bare soles. They were catching up to her. Calling on her gift, she almost screamed in frustration as the foggy, drunken feeling she'd woken with dampened her effort.

She could hear them getting closer, yet she couldn't make her legs move any faster. There was nowhere to hide they wouldn't find her, not with their sense of smell and sight, even in the damp, dark night.

Shifters. Freaking Shifters had found her and taken her as she'd walked home from work. She'd stayed in areas highly populated with humans in hopes of blending in and staying far away from the creatures. They'd risked discovery and for what? Money.

Hollyn knew far too well how much her kind was worth on the trafficking circuit. Even if the humans who bought her didn't know what she was, the energy she put out mixed with her unique looks would intrigue them enough to keep her as their own personal slave.

And then there were the Shifters who'd pay a pretty penny for her womb. There was no evidence of what kind of children an Elemental Fae and Shifter would create, but some believed it would create some kind of super creature, someone able to blend in with humans while holding so many gifts. There were even more who believed the mixture of supernatural blood would aid in the takeover of society, something she had zero interest in.

Sounds of someone running came from ahead of her, then something blurred across the area. Hollyn slid to a stop, the force throwing her forward. Hands grabbed her arms and yanked her up. Opening her mouth to release a scream, she gasped when a hand slapped over her mouth and she was yanked against a hard, warm body. He dragged her until they were hidden behind a tree.

Someone appeared in front of her. She could barely make out his face in the dim moonlight appearing through the gaps in drying leaves overhead. He held a finger to his mouth, moving close enough for Hollyn to see his face.

His eyes raised and he looked over her head and around the tree. In one swift motion, she was scooped into the arms of the man holding her, then all three of them were on the move. Hollyn's body barely jostled as trees zoomed past her. They were running way faster than she could on her own. The stranger was taking her away, hopefully away from danger and not from the fire to the frying pan.

And then the trees parted and a car appeared parked on the shoulder. The guy ahead of her yanked the back door open, then dove into the passenger seat as the guy holding her climbed in, depositing Hollyn onto the seat next to him.

Turning to look through the back window as the car drove off, the sound of tires screeching and smell of burning rubber filling her senses, she watched in terror as four massive wolves chased after the vehicle.

They might be fast, but they couldn't keep up. Eventually, they slowed to a stop, raised their heads in the air and howled long and loud.

Adrenaline coursed through her system, warring with whatever she'd been given to knock her out. Her eyes drooped, her muscles burned and all she wanted to do was sleep.

"What's wrong with her?" the driver asked.

"They drugged her," the guy sitting beside her said, lifting one of her lids and shining a light into her pupil. "You still with us?"

"Yeah," she croaked out as she pulled away from the offensive light.

"I need you to try to stay awake for me," he said.

Now that the imminent threat was behind them, the last thing she wanted was to stay awake. She wanted to go to sleep and wake up and this had been nothing more than a nightmare.

"What's your name?" the guy asked, this time lifting her arm and checking her pulse.

"Hollyn," she said, slumping further in her seat. "You a doctor?"

"Something like that," he said. "I'm Aron. That's Brax," he said, motioning to the guy driving. "And that's his brother Daxon. Mason will meet us later."

"You're Shifters," she said. She realized she should be afraid. What if they hadn't rescued her, but were taking her away from their rivals so they could make the money instead?

But that didn't feel right. These guys seemed different. They'd seemed angry when they found her. And Aron was intent on making sure she was healthy and alive. Her magic didn't recoil from them but aided in slowing her heartrate.

"We are," Aron said, lifting his hand and placing it on her forehead.

She swatted his hand away and scooted until she was almost against the other door.

"You're safe, Hollyn. We're not like those fuckers. You're safe," Aron repeated.

Daxon turned and offered her a bottle of water.

"You trying to drug me, too?" she asked, eying the bottle suspiciously.

"It's still sealed," Daxon said, keeping his arm outstretched.

Taking the bottle from him, she held it close to her ear and listened for the crack of the seal. Even when she heard it, she sniffed at the contents, not convinced they didn't poke a hole with a syringe or something.

Aron took the bottle from her hand and tilted it back, taking a large swig. He offered it back to her with his brows raised as if proving to her the water was safe. With one more sniff, she tilted the bottle back and emptied half its contents.

It didn't help the feeling of being stoned, but her mouth was no longer sticky and dry.

"What did they give me?" she slurred. As the adrenaline wore off, the drugs seemed to be affecting her again.

When she'd woken in that musty room, she'd barely been able to get her feet under her. Until she'd heard the male voices outside her room. Pieces of how she'd gotten from the sidewalk outside her apartment to where ever they'd taken her fell into place and she'd climbed through the window, jumping and landing a full story below.

Her ankle throbbed, but she'd run as fast as she could. They'd discovered her escape minutes later and she'd heard as the conversation and voices turned to growls and snarls of their beasts. If she'd had any doubt about who'd kidnapped her before, those doubts were laid to rest within seconds.

Bending forward, Hollyn touched the swollen area around her ankle. It wasn't broken, but she knew she'd feel it tomorrow.

"What's wrong?" Aron asked, turning the flashlight on his phone and shining it on her foot.

"I turned my ankle when I jumped out the window," Hollyn said, examining the swelling now that she could see.

"You jumped out a window?" Brax asked, glancing at her in the rearview mirror.

"It was either that or try to fight through the assholes who were hanging around outside my door."

All three men chuckled, but Aron kept examining her ankle.

"It's not broken. I'll wrap it when we get somewhere safe."

She heard him, felt the pain of him poking and prodding the bone, but reality was beginning to fade. She knew Aron wanted her to stay awake, but within minutes, she lost the fight with consciousness and sunk into a nightmare about teeth and claws and slavery.

****

Noah groaned as someone pounded on his front door. The sound echoed through the house and felt like a sledgehammer to his skull. Cracking one eye open, he shook his head at the dim light coming through his curtains. It wasn't bright enough for it to be time for him to get up. Whoever the fuck was beating on his door so early in the morning could go away.

But the pounding persisted. And it was too loud to be Shawnee waking him up for work. Throwing the blankets off, he stomped to his front door in nothing but his boxer briefs. He yanked the door open, his mouth open to cuss someone out, then snapped it shut when he realized who was standing on his front porch.

"What the fuck are you doing here? Where the fuck have you been?" he growled out to Aron, the Alpha of the Ravenwood Pride.

That asshole and his buddies had been MIA since the attack on Big River the year before.

"I need a favor," Aron said instead of answering either of Noah's questions.

"Dude, I haven't seen you in a year and you just show up at…what fucking time is it?"

"I've been busy." Aron turned and waved at a woman who stood beside Aron's expensive as fuck sports car.

"Who's that?" Noah asked as the woman approached.

She had hair so black it was almost blue and it hung to the middle of her back, swaying with each step. As she got closer, she pulled it back at her nape and wrapped a rubber band around it, her eyes never leaving his. And those fucking eyes…

The only color that came to Noah's mind was sapphire. He'd always thought Emory from Big River had unique eyes, but she had nothing on this woman. But as she drew near, those eyes seemed to change, lightening until they were the color of the sky. That was no trick of light. And he wasn't tired enough to be seeing shit.

This woman was not human. Yet, he didn't smell fur or anything that would indicate she was a Shifter, either.

Narrowing his eyes on the woman, he turned back to Aron. "What kind of favor?"

They had finally gotten a little peace after Shawnee's family Pride had attacked and tried to drag Shawnee back when she didn't perform the way they thought she should. Was Aron bringing more bull shit to their doorstep?

The woman stopped at the bottom of Noah's steps and looked around at the other cabins before turning her attention back to Noah.

"This is Hollyn. I need you to keep her safe for a while. I'll come back for her later."

Aron turned and started climbing down the steps.

"Wait! What the fuck are you talking about?" Noah moved until he was standing at the top looking down at Aron and Hollyn.

"Keep her safe. That's all I'm asking," Aron said.

"Safe from who?" Noah looked the woman over again and couldn't help but notice her tiny waist, round hips and perky tits. Did she have some kind of ex stalking her or something? And why the hell would Aron bring her to Blackwater? They weren't fucking bodyguards.

"We found her outside of Kansas City. Traffickers snatched her off the street."

Aron's eyes held a faint glow as he spoke making Noah wonder who Hollyn was to him and why he wouldn't just keep her safe himself. The panther and his Pride were perfectly capable of protecting one woman. Why bring her all the way across the state?

Noah looked at Hollyn again. She was almost six inches shorter than Aron putting her somewhere around five foot seven. She was tall compared to the rest of the women in his life.

"They'll still be looking for her. I need you to keep her here until I can find the fuckers and end the threat." Aron's eyes flashed brighter as he spoke. End the threat. He didn't need to spell it out for Noah to know he meant execute the sick bastards.

"Why me?" Noah called after Aron as he made his way to his little sports car.

Aron turned and shrugged. "You were home."

Noah looked around. Everyone was up and gone except him and Shawnee. And since she didn't have a car yet, Aron wouldn't know she was still sleeping inside the cabin she shared with Colton.

"Fuck," Noah muttered as Aron dropped into his car.

He stood with his hands on his hips watching as the gravel threw up dust from Aron's tires. Then, he turned to Hollyn. "I'm Noah," he grumbled and jerked his head toward his house, assuming the woman would follow him inside.

He should've told Aron no. Told him to take the woman somewhere else. Told him they needed a break from all the bull shit. But he didn't. And he wouldn't. Aron and the rest of the panthers had come to their aid when they needed it. They'd helped to keep Big River's mates and the pups safe when a rival wolf Pack had attacked. Technically, Noah owed Aron.

Once Noah was in his kitchen making coffee, he turned to find Hollyn standing barely inside the door, her hands clenched around the strap of a backpack hanging off one shoulder.

"Close the door," he grumbled as he pulled two mugs from the sink and handwashed them. Had it just been him, he'd have rinsed the old coffee out and refilled it.

Hollyn turned and closed the door but she didn't move further into the house.

"You can come in. You want cream and sugar?" he asked as he poured the coffee.

"Are you a Shifter, too?" she asked, her voice a little on the deep side but feminine enough to make his dick twitch.

Noah glanced down at himself. Fuck. He'd had that entire conversation in nothing but his boxers. "I got to get ready for work. Make yourself at home."

He set her mug on the counter, set the sugar container next to it, then left Hollyn standing there as he headed for the shower.

Once he was cleaned up and dressed, he headed back to find Hollyn standing in the kitchen clutching the coffee mug between both hands.

"I'm not going to hurt you," he said, sitting on the couch to pull on his boots.

"You didn't answer my question," she said, watching his every move.

"What question?"

"Are you a Shifter, too?" Her voice was a little louder this time, a little more confident.

Noah looked up from tying his boots and finally noticed the fear in those weirdly gorgeous eyes. "Yeah," he said and turned back to his boots.

He wanted her to see he was normal, safe, not some monster ready to pounce on her.

"Are you like them?"

"Am I a kidnapping piece of shit who thinks a woman is a piece of property? Hell no." He stood and moved to grab his cup of coffee that was probably lukewarm by now.

"That, too. But are you a wolf?"

"Nope. Bear."

"Good," she said with a heavy sigh.

"But my friends are."

And she was back to being tense.

Noah leaned his hip against the counter and really looked at her. There were faint scars on the sides of her face and neck as well her arms. He'd only seen her move when she was outside and she seemed to have a slight limp.

"Are you injured?" he asked, anger rising deep inside of him at the thought of someone touching Hollyn.

Her head wagged slightly side to side, but she never took her eyes off him, even when she sipped at her coffee. It was as if she was afraid the second she looked away, he'd attack her.

"Listen," he said, downing the rest of his bitter, cold drink and dropping it in the sink. "Those assholes that you met? We're not like that. Most Shifters just want to live their life in peace, just like you. We're different. My friends, even the wolves, are different. We fight to protect people, especially females."

His Clan, Big River Pack, and Ravenwood Pride had all gone to war to protect Emory, a wolf and member of Big River, and Callie, a lioness from a piece of shit Pride from forced mating. Since then, the laws had been changed and women were being treated better. Fairly. As equals. The way he was raised and the way it should've been the whole fucking time.

"That's what Aron said," she said, grimacing after taking a drink. He had no idea whether she'd added anything or if she was making the face because her coffee had grown cold, too.

"He's a smart man. I have to go to work." He looked around his pig sty of a house. Fuck. He couldn't just leave her alone all day. Not that he worried she'd touch his shit or steal anything. But Aron worried about her safety. He'd driven over three hours to bring her to Blackwater. How the hell could he watch over her if she was alone in the territory all day.

"You scared of lion Shifters, too?" he asked, only half teasing.

Shawnee was a lioness and mate to one of his Clan brothers. She was also tiny and unimposing.

"Is he as big as you?" she asked, a curve at the corners of her lips.

Ohhh. She was teasing. That was way better than being terrified of him. A little tinge of masculine pride hit him when a pretty pink washed over her cheeks and she dropped her eyes. Had she been flirting and was now embarrassed? And why did he care if she was flirting? She meant something to Aron.

Even as he tried to convince himself she was off-limits, his eyes dipped to the swell of her tits before rising to her face. She'd caught him checking her out. Dammit.

Instead of doing the whole my-eyes-are-up-here deal, she shook her head and smiled. "Don't worry. It happens a lot," she teased.

Okay. So two things happened at her statement. His eyes involuntarily dropped to her chest again, because obviously, they were fucking magnets to his eyeballs. And a wave of jealousy burned his gut at the thought of another man looking at her.

He had to get the fuck out of the house and away from her. Now.

"She's not even as big as you. But she's a Shifter and strong. And she can text any of us if shit goes down. Someone can be here within five minutes."

Shawnee was going to be pissed that she couldn't go to work. If she had her way, she'd work seven days a week right along with Noah. Everyone had given him shit for years, telling him to hire someone else so he could take a day off every once in a while. He'd hired Shawnee, but she waited tables. And no fucking way would he leave her alone all day with a bunch of drunk Shifter idiots.

He held his phone in his hand, thumb poised over the letters, but he was having a hell of a time typing anything. He hated the thought of leaving Hollyn behind. Which made zero fucking sense. Up until about twenty minutes ago, he didn't even know she existed. He knew Shawnee could keep her safe in the time it would take one of the bears or wolves to get to her if there was any trouble.

Then there was another thought: Why the fuck did the traffickers want her so badly Aron thought they'd travel across the state to find her?

"You're not human," he said, dropping his arm back to his side. She continued to stare at him, but he could smell the fear coming from her. "What are you? Why does Aron think those fuckers will keep looking for you?"

Again, she didn't answer, just kept staring at him until her eyes flicked to the door behind him then back. She was thinking of running. No way. He was supposed to keep her safe. And he sure as fuck wouldn't let her run away without a few answers. Was her presence going to put the people he loved in danger?

Noah took a step toward her and she lifted her hand. Her sapphire eyes swirled until they were closer to onyx with specks of silver.

"What – "

Her hand turned over as if she were cupping something and a ball of flame grew and danced, the flames licking the air as if looking for something to destroy.

She was a fucking Fairy. Not just any Fairy, but an Elemental Fairy. She had a strong ass blood line if she was able to call on her talent so easily.

So then how the hell did anyone get their hands on her to begin with?

The flame began to die until she balled her hand in a fist, closing the rest of it off from sight. "I was walking home from work. By the time I heard someone behind me, they stuck me with a needle. And then I woke up on a stained, nasty, stinky bed in a room I didn't know."

That explained how they'd captured someone so powerful. The drugs had probably kept her too weak to fight once she'd woken.

"Does Aron know?"

She nodded once, distrust evident in those oddly beautiful swirling eyes.

"You're safe here, Hollyn. I swear to you, no one will hurt you. I'd give my own life before I allowed that." His bear stretched in his head, finally waking up enough to pay attention. His statement about protecting her with his life felt right, natural, as if there had never been a doubt about it, even before he'd spoken the words.

Hollyn crossed her arms and nodded as if finally believing him. "You said you had to go to work," she said.

Steps sounded on his porch seconds before Shawnee knocked on the door. She was used to him being the one to call for her to get outside. She was probably confused as to why he wasn't ready.

Hollyn's eyes darted to the front door.

"It's just Shawnee. The lion I told you about."

Returning her attention to Noah, her eyes faded back to their sapphire color and Noah could swear she was beckoning him closer. It felt like she'd tied a rope around his dick and was reeling him in.

She's Fae. It's just her magic, he had to remind himself. His dick, however, didn't get the memo.

He'd heard the rumors of the Fae magic, of their pull. Unfortunately, that pull worked against them now that so many of them stayed in hiding. And, after finding out what happened to Hollyn, they had damn good reason to.

Hollyn inhaled sharply, dropped her eyes to the side and took a step back. She must've felt her magic tugging at him, too. Stepping through the living room, he pulled open the door and let Shawnee inside.

Her eyes immediately moved to Hollyn, then she looked at Noah with a confused frown.

How much should he tell Shawnee? He'd been freaked out about leaving her alone and unprotected, but by her small show of power, it was evident she could protect herself if she wasn't outnumbered. Or fucking drugged.

Yet, his beast rumbled in his head at the thought of Hollyn alone. And he wasn't sure she'd want to hang out at a bar all fucking day.

"You mind hanging out here today?" Noah asked, glancing over his shoulder at Hollyn. She hadn't moved, but she was watching them both closely and listening to every word they said.

"Why?" Shawnee asked, her eyes flicking over to Hollyn again. "Who is that?" she whispered low enough that a human wouldn't be able to hear. Hollyn was no human, but he had no idea how keen her hearing was.

Lowering his voice to barely above a whisper, Noah explained who she was and why she was there. With each word he said to

Shawnee, her eyes widened, and her breath came in quick pants. She was pissed.

"They're still looking for her?" Shawnee asked, her voice a little louder.

"You two realize I can still hear you, right?" Hollyn said, answering Noah's internal question as to whether she had supernatural hearing or not.

Noah turned and shrugged. "Wasn't sure you'd want me to rehash all that shit or not."

"So you whispered it? You still rehashed it."

For some reason, her smart ass reply made him smile. She was kind of funny. And sassy as hell. Even through fear and whatever trauma she'd dealt with before Aron had found her, she still carried so much strength and still had her dignity.

And then a thought crossed his mind – had any of those fuckers touched her? Had they sexually assaulted her?

A rage burned hot in his gut and made his bear scratch at his skin to get out. His beast wanted to seek out whoever the fuck dared touch what belonged to him and kill him.

Noah's breath caught in his lungs. *Belonged to him*? Where the fuck had that come from? Hollyn didn't belong to him. She didn't belong to anyone.

"I just need you to hang out for a while until the rest of the guys get home."

"You're not letting me work today?" Shawnee pouted, slapping her hands on her hips.

"Just today. You realize you don't have to work every fucking day, right?"

"Why not? You do," she said with a smirk and one raised brow.

At least the banter with Shawnee calmed the rage simmering just below the surface. No way would he do anything to freak either of these women out, including an uncontrolled Shift.

"You cool with Shawnee hanging out? I promise she won't eat you or try to sell you off," Noah said.

"Not funny," Shawnee muttered under her breath.

"Eh. It was a little funny," Hollyn said.

"Seriously, though. I promise not to go all furry on you or anything. Most of us aren't psychos," Shawnee said with a smile.

"It's fine. I know the drill. Stay inside, lock the doors. Don't open it for anyone," Hollyn said, still standing in the kitchen with the cold cup of coffee clutched between her hands.

"Help yourself to whatever if you get hungry. Do you have a phone?" Hollyn shook her head. "Shawnee does. Either of you text me if you need me. Any of us can get to you within a few minutes."

"We'll be fine," Shawnee assured him with another wide smile for Hollyn.

"Why do you look so insane right now?" Noah grumbled.

"What?"

He imitated her wide, Joker-like grin.

"I was trying to look nice." Shawnee playfully slapped Noah's arm. "Jerk."

"One of these days, I'm going to fire you," Noah teased back as he made his way through the door.

"No, you won't," Shawnee called after him as he pulled the door shut behind him.

He fucking hated leaving Hollyn with just Shawnee. But she had gifts and could probably burn a fucker alive if they came after her. And he had to remember she wasn't his. He was just keeping her safe until Aron came and got her and took her back to her life.

Where did she live before all this? Was it Kansas City? Was that why Aron had found her there? Or had she been taken there? And did she have a family, a job, friends? A boyfriend?

Noah pushed that last thought aside. He didn't like the feeling that slithered through his gut again at the thought of another man touching her, even if she wanted him to. But he couldn't help but wonder if anyone was looking for her. He knew if Hollyn was his, he'd burn the planet down to find her and bring her home.

The further Noah drove his truck from his cabin, the more anxious he grew. His chest felt tight and his heart was beating too fast. Could Shifters have heart attacks? Because he was pretty sure that was what he was feeling.

He glanced in his rearview mirror as the edge of his cabin disappeared behind the trees and he had to fight both himself and his bear from turning the truck around.

Was this just a remnant of her Fae appeal? The glamour, that energy that attracted others to her kind? And how the fuck did she hide that shit in public?

As if she was speaking in his mind, Noah had the answer. She stayed hidden amongst humans. They'd feel that pull, but they'd just think it was her charisma, or blame it on her beauty for the reason they wanted to be near her.

But he really didn't think that was what was happening at that moment. He was too far for it to affect him. Yet, he felt like a rubber band was being stretched until he was uncomfortable.

As intriguing and hot as Hollyn was, he really hoped Aron came and got her soon. Because if she stayed in his house too long…he'd end up falling hard for her.

Already, his gums ached with the need to Shift his teeth and mark her as his forever.

Chapter Two

Hollyn watched the short redhead move around Noah's cabin. There was a tiny crease as she wrinkled her nose.

"I've never been in here before," Shawnee said when Hollyn frowned at her. "He's kind of a slob."

"You've never been in Noah's house?" Hollyn asked. Warring emotions surprised the crap out of Hollyn. She was surprised someone who was part of his family had never seen the inside of his house. And she was relieved another woman hadn't been in there. At least not the beautiful woman checking out the clothes and empty pizza boxes everywhere.

"So, um, does Noah have a girlfriend? Is she going to be jealous I'm here?"

Hollyn turned to set the coffee mug down and squeezed her eyes shut. How freaking pathetic could she sound? There was no denying her attraction toward Noah, even if he was a Shifter. There was something about him that made her want to just climb him like a tree, wrap her legs around him, and enjoy the ride.

As heat rushed her cheeks, she pressed her cool hands to them before turning back around.

"Noah doesn't have a girlfriend," Shawnee said. She didn't sound suspicious or teasing.

When Hollyn looked back at the woman Noah had said was a lion, she smiled when she realized Shawnee was tidying up. She'd collected a few shirts and piled them on the arm of the chair. Raising one to her nose, she yanked the shirt back and grimaced.

"Don't suppose you know where his laundry room is," Shawnee said, holding the cotton in her finger and thumb and well away from her face.

"I know where the living room and kitchen is," Hollyn said with a shrug.

She'd been too scared to move when she'd first gotten there. She'd grown to trust Aron and the rest of the panther men in the two weeks she'd been with them. But it had taken almost the full two weeks for that trust to grow. She'd just met Noah. And the dude was huge. And intense. And had a thick, dark beard that just begged to be touched. No wait. That wasn't right. It was scary. Yeah. She was scared of him.

Shit.

She wasn't scared of him. Not now. Not after about ten minutes of him doing everything he could to put her at ease. She hadn't missed how Noah had kept distance between them, or how he'd made her coffee and set it on the counter for her to take when she wanted. He'd even left her alone in his home while he showered. He'd trusted her not to touch anything or run through the door.

All that, and he was gorgeous. And he called to her gift and made her want to wrap them in a cocoon of flames. That was the part that scared her. The dude wasn't even human.

Then again, neither was she. She was one of the few remaining pure-blood Elemental Fae. Which was why she was worth so much damn money.

Thirty-three years she'd been able to stay under the radar. Thirty-three years of staying anonymous and off the paranormal map. And not only had she been found and kidnapped, she'd been thrust nose deep into the same world she'd tried to hide from her whole life.

"How can he live like this?" Shawnee said as she grabbed a stack of pizza boxes taller than her and carried them outside.

Well damn. She couldn't just stand around and watch Shawnee clean. She should help. Yet, she felt weird touching Noah's stuff. For some reason, it felt overly intimate as she piled Noah's clothes in her arms and sought out his washer and dryer.

When she found the laundry room off the kitchen, she stood in awe. It was spotless. Of course it was; it was obviously never used.

Throwing a stack of dark shirts and jeans into the wash, she started a load of clothes and headed into the kitchen. He had a dishwasher. Why the hell didn't he use it? The entire sink was filled with dirty dishes. She had a feeling him washing her coffee mug was the first time he'd washed a dish in a while.

As she filled the dishwasher until she couldn't find anything else, she turned and looked for Shawnee. She was wiping down the coffee table. All this cleaning felt so domestic. And comfortable.

She should feel awkward cleaning a stranger's house, touching his clothing, standing in his kitchen as if she'd done it a hundred times. But she didn't. For a brief second, she felt at home.

Maybe staying with Noah wasn't a good idea. Surely, Aron had other friends he trusted enough to keep her safe. The town they'd driven through to get to this place had been tiny. Mainly small mom and pop shops and a lot of trees and fields. She was pretty damn hidden in little bitty Cedar Hill, Missouri. Especially tucked away in the bears' territory. Even if he'd deposited her in the middle of town, she'd still be pretty much off the radar. Everyone she'd seen looked like blue-collar workers, construction workers, farmers. And most importantly, human. None of them seemed the kind to sell living, breathing people for money.

"I think that's the best we can do for now," Shawnee said, tossing the dirty towel toward Hollyn as if they were old friends.

Hollyn carried the rag to the laundry room and threw it in the basket with the light-colored clothes. Then she joined Shawnee who stood with her hands on her hips surveying their effort.

"How does it not smell in here with all that crap?" Shawnee said, turning in a slow circle.

"It was messy. Not dirty," Hollyn said, and realized how at ease she was around the female already.

Were the rest of their friends like them? Were Noah's brothers as big and intimidating as him?

"How many of you live here?" Hollyn said, following Shawnee's lead and sitting at the wooden table in the kitchen.

"There's me and Colton. He's my husband. Noah, Luke, and Carter."

"You're the only woman?" Hollyn asked. For some reason, the thought of only two women living amongst four big ass men spooked her a little.

"Yeah. For now. I'm determined to get the rest of them paired up. I can't wait until we have cubs running around here like Big River."

"Big River are the wolves?"

"Yep. Well, there are wolves, a coyote mix, a lioness, and a male lion. Technically, though, the lion and his mate live up the hill."

"What hill?"

Shawnee was rambling on as if Hollyn had a clue what she was talking about.

"Girl. There is so much to tell you," Shawnee said, pushing a rogue curl out of her face. "There's a whole Pride of lionesses living just up the hill from the wolves. Big River, Blackwater, and Ravenwood fought for their freedom. When Eli, that's Emory's mate – "

"I don't know who Emory is," Hollyn said.

"You will. You'll meet all of them if you're here long enough. They all like to hang out as much as possible. Anyway, when Eli left his Pride, he became the Alpha of Hope Pride. That's the group of lionesses I told you about."

Shawnee was chatty, but there was sadness in her eyes as she spoke of the lionesses. Hollyn opened her mouth to ask her if they'd been her friends, but her phone chirped a few times.

"Excuse me," Shawnee said, lifting the phone to her ear. "Hey sexy," she cooed over the line.

Hollyn looked away and gave Shawnee as much privacy as she could while still sitting at the same table. She tried to ignore the lovey-dovey talk until she heard her name mentioned.

"She's a friend of Noah's…no, I'll tell you about it when you get home…well, then, hurry…I will…we're fine," Shawnee said with a chuckle. "I love you, too. Nope. I love you more. Oh, shut up. I'll see you later." She ended the call and set the phone on the table. "That was my husband."

"I assumed," Hollyn said with a genuine smile. That conversation had been a little cheesy but so sweet.

Shawnee gently ran a finger across the screen of her phone with a wistful smile and Noah's mind flashed through Hollyn's mind.

With a hard shake of her head, she tried to erase his face from her mind. Part of her knew exactly what was going on; her magic was trying to show her what Noah was meant to be to her. But he was a

Shifter. Not human. Not Fae. Her life was supposed to be way different. And since she had no idea what kind of children they would have, not to mention the kind of life they'd lead, she refused to acknowledge her fate.

"What?" Shawnee said with a frown.

"Nothing. Just thinking."

"About Noah?" Shawnee said with a raised brow as her lips curved up slowly. "I'm just saying, I saw how you two looked at each other. And he's single. And he's a super great guy. He gave me a job when I had zero education or work experience. And he's so cute with the Big River cubs."

Hollyn held up her hand. "I'm just here until Aron says it's safe for me to go home."

"You could stay," Shawnee said with a shrug, her tone light as if she were just offering a suggestion. But Hollyn could see how badly Shawnee wanted her Clan family to be happy and paired up.

Even if Hollyn hadn't grown up around Shifters, she knew all about their mate bond, how women were forced to be paired up with men they didn't choose, and she'd even heard that the laws had changed. Aron had mentioned something about knowing the people responsible for those changes, but he'd never mentioned he'd been a big part of it, as well.

Noah had been a part of that fight. The man grumbled a lot and seemed to try really hard to make people think he was this big, grumpy guy, but anyone who would risk their own life for not just those he loved, but for women he'd never met was a good guy in Hollyn's eyes.

She had to get him off her mind before she encouraged her magic. When it had swelled and reached for Noah, he'd definitely felt it. She'd seen him take a step closer as his eyes widened the slightest bit. When he'd turned to leave, he looked like he was fighting the pull, straining with every step to walk away from her.

How much did he know about her kind? Was he aware of what had happened? Maybe he thought she was glamouring him. Not her style. Although, she'd never been shy about using that energy she was born with to encourage men and women both to tip her well. They probably got home each night and tried to figure out where the intense attraction came from and where the hell their money had gone.

Not her proudest moment, but a girl had to make a living. She'd tended bar in so many towns since she'd turned twenty-one. She was damn good at it, too. Because of her magic, she was able to perform the tricks only the masters knew how to do. And she loved to use her fire magic and blow the flaming alcohol from her mouth. Or at least the humans thought it was flaming alcohol.

Shawnee tapped on her screen, this time sending out a text. Hollyn tried to be as inconspicuous as possible while reading what she was writing. Just because she was comfortable with the sweet redhead didn't mean she fully trusted her.

"I'm just letting Noah know he's a slob and that we're coming for lunch," Shawnee said, her eyes still glued to her screen. She finished and turned the screen for Hollyn to see. Either Shawnee could see Hollyn trying to read her message or she had the same issues with trust as Hollyn did.

"We're going to his work?"

"He owns a bar. That's where I work. I wait tables for him so he can, I don't know, not do every single thing himself. We've been trying to convince him to hire more people so he can take the day off every once in a while."

Shawnee stood and rounded the table. "You coming?"

"It isn't lunch time," Hollyn said, standing and following her out the door. They stepped out and Hollyn looked around. Did Shawnee expect them to walk, because there wasn't a single vehicle parked outside.

"A couple of the women from Big River are coming to get us," Shawnee said when she saw Hollyn's confused frown. "You'll love them. Just a heads up, though, Nova tends to say the first thing that pops in her head."

Okay then. More chatty women and at least one of them didn't have a filter. Honestly, though, she was excited to be around more females. She'd been locked up with the four panthers for the last couple of weeks and hadn't seen another woman until Shawnee had come to the door.

"Are they all…"

"Shifters?"

"Yeah."

"Yep. Let's see," Shawnee said as she waited on the porch. "I'm not sure who's coming but Nova, Emory, Lola, and Peyton are all wolves. Callie's a lion like me, though."

More wolves. Noah and Shawnee had told her a few times that Shifters weren't like the assholes who'd drugged her and snatched her off the street. Even with those reassurances, the fact she'd be in the car with more wolves, just like the aforementioned assholes, made her heart race faster and her palms sweat.

"I promise it'll be fine. You'll love everyone," Shawnee said, raising her hand in a short wave when a small vehicle bumped into view.

And then another followed.

"Looks like you'll meet all the girls," Shawnee said as she descended the stairs.

Her anxiety kicked into high gear as women poured out of the two vehicles.

"We didn't have a sitter. Dad went into town," a dark-haired woman with curves like Shawnee said as Shawnee peeked into the backseat. "Hi. I'm Nova," she said, her hand outstretched toward Hollyn as she closed the space between them.

"Hollyn," she said, taking Nova's offered hand.

"We going to have another wedding soon?" Nova asked, a wide grin splitting her face.

Hollyn pulled her hand away and turned wide eyes to Shawnee. What had the woman told everyone?

"No. Nothing like that," Hollyn reassured her.

"It's a long story," Shawnee jumped in. "She's just visiting. She's a friend of Aron's."

"From Ravenwood?" a pink-haired woman asked.

"Yeah," Hollyn said, following the women to the vehicles.

"You're riding with me," Nova said. "I've got questions."

"Leave her alone," a petite woman said with a wide grin. "I'm Emory. That's Lola," she motioned to the pink-haired woman who climbed in beside one of the car seats holding a toddler who looked to be just under two. "That's Peyton," she motioned to a woman with white blonde hair and purple streaks. "And the quiet one is Callie."

"Hi," the blonde who was barely an inch taller than Emory said.

"Don't be mad if I ask your names ten more times," Hollyn said, taking the front seat in Emory's car while Shawnee climbed into Nova's.

"Girl, just wait until you meet all our mates. There are a lot of us," Emory said as she pulled the car out of the spot in front of Noah's cabin and followed Nova's car down the bumpy, gravel road.

And once again, her anxiety grew even more. By the time they got to Noah, she'd be bordering on a panic attack.

The thought of seeing Noah calmed her nerves while sending butterflies abuzz in her stomach. Such a strange sensation to be calmed and unnerved by a man, all at the same time.

Emory chattered on about the guys in her Pack, pointed out various locations for her to shop, and told her more about the bears. Hollyn watched the scenery pass her by, trying her best not to snort at the limited selection of stores. She perked up when Emory got to the gossip about Noah.

"He's been single as long as I've known him. He pretty much works twenty-four/seven, so I'm sure he doesn't have much time to meet women."

No matter how much Hollyn tried to convince these women she'd be leaving soon, they were all intent on playing Cupid with their friend.

As pushy as they were, it was kind of sweet. They obviously cared a lot about Noah. It just reaffirmed Aron's insistence that Shifters were just like humans, except for the animal inside of them. They formed bonds, fell in love, grew families. They had friends and liked to play. They worked and paid bills, although theirs were paid with cash and all their bills were under false names.

Aron had filled in the gaps for her that she didn't know on her own. Maybe he knew she'd be immersed in the Shifter world for longer than a few weeks.

The trees and fields faded to buildings and fast food joints. Emory turned the car right and Hollyn watched all the tiny shops pass her by. Was this what the local people referred to as going into town?

Emory pulled into a gravel parking lot in front of a long, unassuming, white building. There were a couple of trucks and one car parked along the front. This was a bar? It looked like a rundown house that was out of place.

All the women piled out of the cars, so Hollyn did, too. She followed them into the place, squinting when they stepped into the dimly lit, smoky room. "You guys still smoke inside?"

Emory gave her a disgusted look and shrugged. "Some places in this county still allow it. You'll get used to showering when you leave."

Hollyn looked around the room, taking in everything from the large number of tables, to where the few patrons were sitting, then finally, and most importantly, the exits.

Until her eyes landed on Noah.

"What the hell are you all doing here?" Noah grumbled, his dark brows pulled together.

"I told you I was bringing Hollyn for lunch. How did you think I was going to get her here? Shift and carry her on my back?" Shawnee said, pulling out a chair at the table closest to the bar.

Noah came around the bar and leaned down close to Shawnee. "She's supposed to be staying under the radar. You just introduced her to the entire freaking wolf Pack," he said, a light growl to his words.

Shawnee didn't look nervous, but Hollyn sure was feeling it.

"Not the whole Pack," Nova said. "Want me to text Gray and get the rest of the guys down here for lunch?" she offered.

"For the love of God," Noah said, throwing his hands in the air. "No. I don't want all those jackasses down here right now. What do you guys want?"

Noah nodded as each woman ordered, but Hollyn hadn't even looked at the menu. She'd been too busy staring at the large male who kept glancing in her direction every few seconds as if making sure she was still there.

****

It'd been hard as hell for Noah to leave Hollyn at his place. That rubber band stretching feeling never faded. And he could've sworn he'd known the second she'd pulled into the parking lot of his place. He'd finally felt a little relief.

When Shawnee told Noah they were coming up for lunch, he'd stupidly assumed Colton was picking them up. He didn't think for a second every single female member of Big River would walk through the door with her.

If she was scared, she sure as hell didn't look it. In fact, she'd barely looked away from him since she'd walked through the door. He knew the feeling; he was having a hard time keeping his eyes off her.

Once he had everyone else's orders, he turned to Hollyn to find her still watching him. And once again, he wondered if she was using magic on him. He fought his feet from moving closer. Fought his hands from reaching out and touching her. There would be no reason for her to intentionally pull him to her; did she even realize she was doing it?

Noah pushed through the doors to the kitchen and started everyone's food. And once again, he fought against the urge to walk back through the swinging doors and scoop Hollyn into his arms.

He'd found her attractive from the second he'd laid eyes on her. This…whatever the hell was going on didn't really hit him until she'd began to settle into his home a little and seemed to accept her current situation. That situation being thrust into a world she tried to hide from, on the run from sick fucks, and living with a complete stranger.

The question of whether she had a boyfriend stayed right there in the front of his mind. There was no way. Aron or Hollyn would've mentioned it. They would've included him in her hiding, or he'd have been the one to protect her. Aaaand there was that green fog in his gut again.

He had no right to be jealous or possessive, but yeah, he was feeling both. And so was his bear.

Noah grinned when he heard the women laughing, including an unfamiliar feminine laugh. Unfamiliar to his ears, but his body and heart knew whose throaty, sexy sound that was. And that fact scared the fuck out of him. Everything about Hollyn scared him. No. Not everything about Hollyn. It was the way he was already obsessed with the woman he knew less than a fucking day.

Did it really matter how long it had been, though? If his bear chose her, did it matter whether he'd known her a year or an hour?

"What the fuck?" Noah said, looking up from the food sizzling on the grill. What the fuck was he even thinking? He couldn't mate with this woman. She would be gone, out of his life forever soon. As soon as Aron thought she was safe, he'd come steal Hollyn away and Noah would never see her again. He had to remember that. He had to remember she was temporary.

Plating all their food in different baskets, he almost slammed into Shawnee as he pushed through the door, all the food on a tray.

"Want me to get it?" she asked, a wide grin on her face, an innocent look in her eyes.

"No, I don't want you to get it. You're off today. Go. Sit," he ordered. He knew what the little redhead was doing. She thought if she brought Hollyn to the bar, Noah would let her work. Since she was already there and all.

Shawnee poked her tongue out at him, stomped her foot, and turned to head back to the table. Noah set each order in front of the correct person – he'd been doing it long enough he no longer needed to write shit down – then set Hollyn's down. She'd ordered a burger, medium rare, no pickles, with a side of fries.

And then he hovered like a weirdo.

"Why don't you sit with us a while," Nova said, wagging her eyebrows up and down when Hollyn wasn't looking.

Noah's eyes darted to Hollyn then back. Either Nova was doing like Shawnee usually did and trying to get him paired up, or he was being overly obvious with his attraction to the sapphire-eyed Fairy.

Hollyn was oblivious.

"I've got work to do," Noah grumbled and carried the empty tray back to the bar.

Really, he didn't have much to do. There were just the two regulars with their asses parked on the same barstools they were every fucking day. Their eyes stayed glued to the TV over the bar even though the sound was down and the jukebox played in the background. He pretended to wipe down the bar top, washed already clean glasses, checked the coolers even though he'd filled them when he got in less than two hours earlier.

Shit. He needed something to look busy. He needed a lunch rush. And as much as he hated to wish it, he really wished the wolves or his Clan brothers would come in and distract him, give him something to cook or drinks to pour.

Anything other than constantly staring at Hollyn through the mirror hanging over the bottles of liquor.

"Hey," Shawnee's voice startled him. Even though she was a cat Shifter and quiet on her feet, she still shouldn't have been able to sneak up on him. He'd been too preoccupied with watching Hollyn's lips close around her burger.

"Just come sit down with us," Shawnee whispered. "We can all see you watching her. Talk to her. Maybe she's your mate," she said, a hopeful lilt to her words.

Noah's eyes widened and jerked over to Hollyn. She wasn't watching him and Shawnee, just nodding as she listened to Callie talk, a small smile tipping the corners of her lips up. And then those lips closed around the straw.

Every fucking thing she did made his dick jump and his brain turn to mush.

He needed to call Aron. Bringing more trouble into his Clan – and marking a Fae who was on the run from traffickers was definitely a shit ton of trouble – was the last thing any of them needed.

Yet, the more he watched her, the more his affection grew toward her, the more his bear paid attention to her, the less he could stand the thought of allowing someone else to protect her. He couldn't just throw her to the wolves, figuratively or literally. She was safe with him, with his Clan, with his friends. Hell, Peyton alone would tear the throat out of anyone who even thought about hurting Hollyn. And Peyton had only just met her. That was how his friends were; they protected the innocent, fought for what was right.

And he'd fight for what was his. Whether he wanted to admit it or not, whether he'd be able to keep her when all this was over or not, whether she had any desire to be in his life or not, she was his.

Noah checked on his two customers at the bar, then the one sitting toward the back finishing up his lunch, and he did something he'd never done in the time he'd owned the bar: he sat down to relax with his friends.

More importantly, he sat down to enjoy a little time with Hollyn.

One day and this woman was turning his life upside down, and as hard as he tried, he was having a hard time hating it.

Chapter Three

Noah eventually followed Shawnee back to the table and sat in a chair across from her. Hollyn tried to keep her eyes on whoever was talking, but the traitorous things kept trailing back to him. There was a light sheen of sweat across his forehead and Hollyn wondered if it was from working in the kitchen making their food, or nerves. Because she totally got the nerves thing. She was just supposed to hang out with him until Aron thought it was safe, but she couldn't stop her mind from wondering what it would be like to stay here, to stay with Aron.

And what it would be like to feel Noah's lips against hers, his hands on her body, his weight pressing down on her from above.

As her cheeks grew warm, she ducked her gaze when Noah glanced at her and caught her staring. Whatever. She'd caught him staring at her a few times, too. And he could chalk it up to curiosity about the woman who'd been forced on him, but her magic told her otherwise.

Every cell in her body was drawn to him, something she knew would one day happen. She just never thought it would happen with a Shifter. Actually, she'd *hoped* it wouldn't happen with a Shifter. Or anyone other than a fellow Fae. Although, the odds of encountering another of her kind was about as good as staying hidden from everyone and everything for the rest of her life. Her kind was more or less endangered for the sole reason that she was hidden; they were hunted, used for others' gain, sold off for large sums of money, and experimented on.

Shame others of her kind, other Elementals hadn't been discovered by someone like Aron and handed over to someone like Noah for protection. Maybe then the story would be different. Maybe then, she'd still have a family.

These people were awful close, like a family. If Noah accepted her, if he accepted the fact her magic had chosen him, if he accepted the fact she was neither human nor Shifter, she would finally have a family. But Noah wasn't the only one who needed to accept their fate.

There were a whole lot of if's in that situation, though.

"So, what do you think? You up for a little shopping?" Nova asked, snapping Hollyn's attention back to the here and now instead of her wishful thinking.

"I don't have any money. I didn't really have anything with me when…well, when Aron found me," Hollyn answered.

"You mean when those jackasses kidnapped you," the blond woman, Peyton, said. And then her eyes glowed an odd turquoise color with a hint of red near her pupils.

"Down, girl," Nova said. "Those assholes are gone and she's safe now. Don't go all Cujo and ruin lunch."

"Cujo?" Hollyn asked, looking from Nova to Peyton and back. "The eighties horror movie?"

"Yep. Our girl, Peyton, tends to go psycho doggie when she gets riled up."

"She's super protective of anyone her animal declares as her Pack," Callie explained with a soft smile. The woman didn't speak much, but when she did, Hollyn couldn't help but give her her attention. Where the other women teased and joked, Callie was quiet and to the point.

"Your animal declared me part of her Pack?" Hollyn asked and smiled at the warm feeling of belonging. Noah, on the other hand, tensed across the table.

Maybe she'd read him wrong. Maybe her magic had chosen wrong. Because he didn't seem to enjoy the thought of Hollyn belonging there any longer than she had to.

"I can buy your stuff," Nova said, going back to the shopping trip. "No one ever lets me buy them stuff anymore."

"Because you have a pup to spoil now," Emory said with a smile as she bent down and made a face at the little girl sitting in a highchair between Emory and Nova.

"I can spoil Rieka and still buy my friends stuff."

"Spending money is her love language," the pink-haired woman, Lola, said with a wink.

"She bought me a house and furnished it before Micah made her stop," Callie said with a nod.

"Your shed was small, and you barely let me buy anything," Nova said on a pout.

"I'm fine. Thanks, though," Hollyn said. As much as she'd love some clothes that hadn't formerly belonged to someone else, and maybe more than three pairs of panties, she didn't want any of these people thinking they had to take care of her. She'd always been independent and didn't plan to change that just because her life had been irrevocably altered.

"You going to get a job?" Shawnee asked.

Noah jumped and frowned over at Shawnee and Hollyn wondered if the little redhead hadn't kicked him under the table.

"Am I allowed to?" Hollyn asked, suddenly hopeful. She'd spent so much time locked in Aron's house, and now she was pretty much locked in Noah's for the unforeseen future. She'd love to get back to her life, or at least a semblance of it. And working would definitely made her feel like herself again.

"Aren't you hiring?" Nova asked Noah with a wide shit-eating grin.

"I—"

"You could definitely use more help around here," Emory said, her smile equally as mischievous as Nova's.

Okay. Did they see what Hollyn's magic detected and were trying their best to shove the two of them together, or did Noah really need a cook or something.

"You have any experience working in a bar?" Shawnee asked, propping her chin on her folded fists.

"I've worked in bars for the last ten years," Hollyn said and looked around at all the wide eyes and grins.

"Can you work behind the bar?" Shawnee asked, glancing at Noah for a brief second before turning her attention back to Hollyn.

"That's the only thing I've done," Hollyn said with a shrug.

Noah was staring at her now with an expression she didn't understand. Doubt? Skepticism? Maybe even interest. She had no idea.

"What do you think, Noah? We could use another bartender. Then, you could take a day off," Shawnee said.

"First of all," Noah said, leaning forward and lowering his voice until Hollyn could barely hear him. "She's supposed to be hiding, not hanging out with a bunch of Shifters."

"Yeah, but you'll be here. And Aron wanted you to protect her, right?" Shawnee said.

Hollyn glanced across the table at Peyton; her eyes were glowing again. "You okay?" Hollyn asked her.

"Yep," Peyton said.

"Don't you dare Shift in here," Noah said, pointing a finger at her with a deep scowl on his face.

Peyton's nostrils flared as she closed her eyes and took a deep breath.

"She's still learning how to control her animal," Emory explained.

"Second of all, don't you think I should be the one to interview her?" Noah asked, glancing at Hollyn. His eyes dipped to her chest before jerking away and Hollyn felt that heat rush her cheeks again. Even if he didn't like the idea of Hollyn being there, even if her magic was wrong – which it never was – he was definitely attracted to her.

"Want me to make you a cocktail to prove it?" Hollyn asked.

Noah held his hands out. "If I hire her to take a day off, how would that be me protecting her?" Noah asked.

"I'll be here," Shawnee said. "And there are always other Shifters in here. If it's more than I can handle and none of our friends are here, it would take you, what, five minutes to get here?"

"Fifteen. Ten if I speed," Noah said, a muscle ticking in his jaw.

"Oh, bull shit. I've seen how fast you boys drive," Nova said, waving her hand dismissively in the air. "And we're in here several times a week for lunch or breakfast. You know almost every single customer that comes in. She'll be fine."

"Aron—" Noah started to say, but Emory cut him off.

"I work right across the street," Emory said. "It would take me no time at all to provide some back up."

"Can you make a Long Island Iced Tea?" Shawnee asked.

"This is my place," Noah said, pushing to his feet. "I decide who works here and who doesn't." He turned his attention to her then closed his eyes slowly, his breathing coming in long, deep pulls as if he was trying to calm down. “Can you make a Long Island Iced Tea?”

Hollyn saw the girls exchange looks from the corner of her eye.

“Sure,” Hollyn said, pushing to her feet and hurrying behind the bar. In no time flat, she had the drink mixed and set it on the bar and waited for Noah to come over and taste it.

Noah looked at each woman as if he were their father and disappointed in them. All but Nova averted their eyes; she just grinned wide at him and batted her lashes. In long strides, Noah moved to the bar and grabbed the glass, ignoring the straw and taking a long drink.

When he set it down, he didn’t say a word, but Hollyn could tell he was impressed.

“What else can you make?” he asked.

Oh. He wanted to see what she could do. *Challenged accepted, big boy.*

Hollyn began to grab bottles, tossing them behind her back before catching them, twirling them in her hands, and doing other tricks she’d learned through the years. By the time she was done, a row of colorful shots waited on the bar for his approval.

The women exploded in applause as Noah grabbed a tiny glass and threw it back. He stared at her for a minute before nodding.

“Fine. But you only work when I’m here.”

“But—” Nova started, but Noah whirled and jabbed a finger in her direction. “Just be happy I’m agreeing to this. I still think it’s a bad fucking idea.”

Hollyn’s smile widened into a full-blown grin. She might not be back at her apartment, she might not be back in the town where she’d lived the last two years, but she’d have a job while she waited for Aron to declare her safe again.

Or until Hollyn’s magic successfully tied Noah to her permanently.

****

Noah bit back the growl when the two old codgers at the bar whistled and cheered at Hollyn’s show. They were merely being polite, excited by something new. Yet, his beast was scratching at Noah to be released. He wanted blood. He wanted to punish the males for looking at Hollyn.

Mate. Mine.

Not a fucking chance. His bear might believe this woman was their mate, but Noah's human half wasn't convinced they weren't attracted to her magic and energy that flowed freely from her now. It was bad enough back at his place; it seemed now that she was focusing on avoiding dropping the bottles, she couldn't focus on reigning in that special whatever it was that pulled people to her.

Even if it was her magic, Noah couldn't keep his eyes off her as she smiled and giggled at all the attention. It was obvious she felt at home behind the bar. She'd said she'd done it for the past ten years; it was something familiar and known to her.

He still wasn't thrilled about the idea of her being the center of attention. He needed to get hold of Aron and see his thoughts on her working the bar. He'd contemplated hiring someone to give him a break occasionally. But if Hollyn was working there, no way could he leave her alone in public like that. No matter how many ideas the women came up with to keep her safe.

Hollyn turned that megawatt grin on Noah and he couldn't help himself; he smiled back. "You're good," he said. No reason he couldn't compliment her on her skill. Especially since she'd apparently spent years honing it.

"Thanks. There's more, but I figured that was enough. So?"

"So what?" he grumbled as he took all the glasses and began to clean them.

"Can I have the job?"

He looked up from the sink and bit back a groan. She'd drawn her bottom lip between her teeth and held it there while she waited for his answer. It was probably a nervous habit, but it just made Noah think about her making that face during sex.

"Let me talk to Aron first," he said and hated the way her smile faded, and sadness entered her eyes.

He'd just reminded her once again how far out of control her like had spiraled.

"But I'm sure it's fine," Noah threw in quickly. He hated that look in her eyes. He loved her smile. And wanted to be the one to make her grin that big more often.

A wave of her magic washed over him and Noah's muscles burned with the strain of keeping his hands to himself. Did she know what she was doing? Did she know she was calling to his animal?

Did she know she was playing with fire?

"Yay! Now, we *have* to go shopping," Nova said. "You've got to have some work clothes. Do you have any makeup?"

"She doesn't need makeup," Noah said, unable to pull his eyes from her face as those waves of warmth radiated from her and washed over him. It was getting harder and harder for him to keep his hands at his sides instead of pulling her close to his chest and burying his face in her hair.

Hollyn's eyes did that swirling thing like back at his house. This time, instead of melting into an onyx color, they faded to a shade of amethyst. It was like her eyes were a mixture of different gems, depending on her mood.

The room grew quiet, but Noah didn't bother looking to see what was going on. He couldn't focus on anything other than the woman who was taking a step closer to him, those beautiful eyes fixated on his lips.

Muscles taut and burning, he slowly reached forward until his fingers grazed her arm. That was all he'd allow himself. He hoped it would settle his beast, but he'd been wrong. It just made him hungry for more.

"What are they doing?" Callie whispered.

Hollyn blinked rapidly a few times and she looked around as if she was confused as to where she was. And those brilliant amethyst eyes bled back to sapphire. Whatever spell they'd been under snapped and Noah shook his head.

He could've blamed her. He could've accused her of glamouring him, putting him under some spell to get a job. But she'd looked just as lost as he did. She'd had no control over whatever the fuck had just happened.

"Give them a minute. I've never seen him act like that," Shawnee whispered so low Noah almost missed it. He doubted Hollyn heard it.

"I, uh..." Hollyn pressed her hands to her cheeks. "Thanks. Let me know what Aron says." She hurried out from behind the bar and made a beeline for her seat at the table.

All the women watched her with raised brows and wide eyes.

"What?" she finally said, looking around at all their faces.

"Nothing," Nova said, blinking and plastering on a fake smile. "Shopping trip? If you won't let me spend my big bucks on you, you can always just pay me back later."

"Big bucks?" Hollyn asked, glancing at Noah before looking away quickly.

"She writes naughty books," Emory said with a smirk.

"I write romance. And people love sexy country boys. They're keeping me rolling in the dough, which in turn, lets me buy my people pretty stuff."

"But I'm not—" Hollyn said, pointing at herself.

"Honey, as long as you're in our territory, you're one of my people."

"She's not in your territory," Noah grumbled, finally getting his wits about him.

"Whatever. She's one of us for now," Nova said, lifting her chin and daring Noah to argue.

He threw his hands up in surrender. Honestly, he liked the thought of the women accepting Hollyn as part of the group. One fucking day and he was ready to go all domestic and make Hollyn his mate.

All the women stood up and threw bills on the table for Noah. He'd refused money for years, chalking it up to feeding his family. But he'd never been able to successfully refuse their tips. They always found creative ways to leave it, so he'd stopped fighting them on it. They didn't know he took every single one of their tips and donated it to the local food pantry.

"Where you going?" Noah asked, instantly nervous.

"Shopping. Keep up, teddy bear," Nova said.

Hollyn frowned at Nova.

"She nicknames everybody. Don't worry; you'll get one, too," Emory said with a roll of her eyes.

"Speaking of, you going to tell us what you are?" Nova asked as they neared the exit.

"Human," Hollyn lied. And not well, either.

"Uh huh," Nova said, not believing her for one second. "That's fine. Keep it a secret. I'll come up with something appropriate."

"Is it just you girls?" Noah asked, leaning on the bar, his palms flat on the surface. He seriously didn't like the thought of just the six women and two babies in Fenton alone.

"Don't be a chauvinist," Nova said with a disappointed shake of her head. "Between Cujo and my wolf, she'll be fine."

"Hey, what about us," Lola said. "Don't worry, Noah. We'll keep her safe. Promise," the pink-haired wolf said with a wink.

All the women filed through the door, but Shawnee lingered a second. "I'll meet you out there," she called to the women.

Nova raised one brow, motioned to Hollyn when her back was turned, then wagged her brows up and down at Noah. Noah shooed her out the door with a deep frown.

When the door closed, Shawnee grew serious. "How much of her is a secret?" she whispered barely above a breath, ensuring the men still in Moe's wouldn't hear her.

"All of it. I don't want anyone to know what she is or where she's from. Don't hang out too long. Just get what she needs and get her home. Here," he said, pulling a couple hundreds from his wallet. "Let her use this. Actually," he said, pulling two more hundred dollar bills out. "Here."

"How much cash do you carry with you?" she said, her eyes wide as she took the money.

"Get what she needs. And make sure she has some comfortable shoes."

Shawnee smiled sweetly up at Noah. "You like her." Noah looked away and wiped the already clean bar. "I like her, too. I think she's perfect for you."

"You just want the Clan paired up. Go. Be safe. Keep Hollyn safe. And call me if there are any problems."

Noah swatted at her with the damp towel and she giggled. "She likes you, too, Noah. I can tell. You two constantly stare at each other."

"It's been one day, Shawnee. Of course we're staring at each other. We have to live together for who-the-fuck knows how long." And she was a beautiful woman with full perky tits, a firm ass, and her Fae magic called to him and his animal.

A small chuckle escaped Shawnee as she patted Noah's arm. "Okay. Fine. Stick with that. In the meantime, we'll be fine. I'll text you when we're headed home."

Shawnee moved toward the door and stopped before stepping out. "We cleaned your house, by the way."

"Why? It was fine the way it was," Noah said.

Shawnee snorted. "It was gross. How the hell do you live like that?"

She pushed through the door, letting sunlight filter in for a brief second before the door closed again. But it was enough for Noah to get another glimpse of Hollyn standing nearby, looking at Emory as she spoke, a pretty smile lighting up her face.

"She's right, you know," one of the codgers at the bar said.

"What the hell you talking about now, John?" Noah said, grabbing his half-empty glass and topping it off at the tap.

"You were staring at that little girl the whole time she was here."

"She's far from a little girl."

Hollyn looked to be in her mid-twenties to early thirties. That made her a few years younger than Noah, but it was hard to tell with Fairies. They aged remarkably well.

"All I'm saying is you'd be a fool if you didn't chase that one out the door," John said as he lifted his glass to his lips.

"You just want me to leave so you'll have free access to my beer," Noah said, but his eyes were on the door.

He heard the cars start up, but they hadn't pulled out yet.

"Fuck," he growled out as he leapt over the bar and ran through the door. What was he doing? What was he even going to say?

Emory's car was still parked and she was watching the door as if expecting Noah to run out. Hollyn leaned against the passenger door, her back to Noah, her arms crossed.

Emory smiled wide, then looked down at her phone to give him a bit of privacy.

"Hollyn," Noah said as he neared the car and rounded the hood. She barely glanced over her shoulder. "Wait."

With a sigh, Hollyn dropped her arms and turned to face Noah as he came closer.

"I..." He still didn't know what to say. But he did have a question. "Are you glamouring me?"

"What?" she asked, her brows pulled low.

"At my house. And in there," he said, hooking his thumb over his shoulder. "Were you glamouring me?"

This time when she sighed, it was a relieved sound. "Then you felt it?"

Shit. He'd been right. And he so fucking didn't want to be right.

"No. I wasn't glamouring you. My magic was calling to you."

It was Noah's turn to frown in confusion. "I don't know what that means."

"How late do you usually get home?" she asked, reaching down to grab the handle to the door.

"Around one or later." She'd be asleep by the time he got home and the last thing he wanted to do was wake her up. He was still exhausted from being woken up so early this morning after being out late.

"We'll talk tonight. It's too much to discuss in the parking lot." She pulled the door open and moved to get in but stopped with her hand on the top of the car. "I wasn't glamouring you," she said again as if making sure he believed her.

He nodded once, setting his hand on the open door as she lowered into the seat. He waited while she pulled on the safety belt, then closed the door softly.

"Be safe," he said after she rolled down her window. "If anything at all seems out of place, stay close to humans and text me. I'll get every single fucking Shifter I know there within minutes."

"We'll take care of her," Emory said.

"We've got her back," Lola said from the backseat, her hand on the chest of her baby.

Six women with two cubs. He hated the thought of them fighting with the baby girls in tow, but all he needed was for them to keep anyone from yanking Hollyn away before he could get to her.

Noah tapped on the top of the car and stood in the parking lot, watching as both vehicles pulled away, sending a cloud of gravel dust into the air.

His mind wandered to Colton, and the men of Big River. Had it happened so quickly for them? Because since the moment he'd laid eyes on Hollyn, he'd had the urge to cover her in his scent, leave his mark, and declare the beautiful blue-eyed woman his. He wanted to keep her safe. He wanted to make her happy.

And he wanted her to stay in his life, even after the risk to her life was over.

Chapter Four

Hollyn followed the ladies around, even carried Rieka a couple of times when the toddler reached her chubby hands out. She hadn't held a baby in years. Hadn't even been around kids in years. Bars weren't exactly known to be child friendly.

"She likes you," Nova said with a smile. "Feel free to babysit anytime." She winked at Hollyn and went back to holding items of clothing up for Hollyn's approval.

Hollyn had never been much into labels, but she liked sparkly things and her favorite color just happened to be pink. And purple. And pretty much every single color of the rainbow. She missed her more feminine pieces. All she'd had were the flannels, t-shirts, and jeans she'd either borrowed from Aron and the rest of the panthers, or what they'd bought her from resale shops. Not that she minded thrift stores, but it would've been nice to pick out her own clothes.

"You're a girly girl, aren't you?" Nova said when Hollyn nodded at a pink sweater that hung off one shoulder.

"Oh yeah. Always have been," Hollyn admitted, handing Rieka back to her mother. It was fun holding her for a minute, but she didn't really know how to play with her. She'd never thought about motherhood because she'd always figured she'd be terrible at it.

"I can't wait to see you all done up for work," Shawnee said. "There's a makeup place here, too, if you want."

"Nah. I can get the drugstore stuff. I'm not into contouring or any of that. Don't really know how," she admitted. She liked eye makeup and lipstick but had never really gotten into foundation or any of the more intricate applications of makeup.

"We can stop on our way back. You need anything else, like a toothbrush or deodorant?" Emory asked, examining the load in the basket. "You better try this stuff on before you buy it. I'm pretty sure Noah was about to have a stroke with us coming here. If you have to make a repeat trip without him, he might have a damn heart attack."

"He's super protective is all," Shawnee said, shooting Emory a dirty look.

"That's what I meant," Emory said, her brows raised in innocence. "All the guys are protective. Just because the laws changed doesn't mean—"

Shawnee jabbed Emory in the ribs with her elbow. "Did you need underwear or bras?"

"I know about the laws and all that," Hollyn said, giving her a soft smile to try to put her at ease. "What I didn't already know before all this, Aron filled me in on the rest. He wanted to make sure I knew how important it was to stay inside the house when he had to leave for whatever reason."

"Oh," Shawnee said. "Sorry," she said to Emory who held a hand to her ribs and frowned at Shawnee.

"And I'm good for now. I don't want to spend too much of Nova's money," Hollyn teased.

"Oh honey," Nova said, sauntering over. "Didn't Red tell you? Your man gave her four hundred smackers to spend on you."

"Nooovaaaa," Shawnee whined.

"Girl, by now you should know if it's a secret, Nova's the last person you tell," Lola said with a shake of her head.

Shawnee still gawked at Nova and shook her head.

"Why would he give me four hundred dollars? And he's not my man." *Yet.*

Thoughts of the conversation she'd promised Noah later that night sent those butterflies abuzz in her belly again. She'd have to be honest. And since he'd felt her magic calling to him, and since he was obviously attracted to her, they had more to discuss than whether or not they should go steady.

Hell, it was more than just the mate bond in his species. Once her magic marked him with its tendrils, there was no going back. For better or worse. And all that stuff.

"You okay?" Shawnee asked, her brows pinched slightly. "You look a little pale."

Of course she did. She was actually considering forever with a man she'd met that day. Not someone she'd known and grown to care about. Not someone who'd originally been a friend. Hell. He wasn't even someone she'd met a few times in passing. They'd literally met each other less than twelve hours ago and she was contemplating following her magic and binding herself to Noah in every way possible.

"I'm fine," Hollyn lied. "Can we still go by a drug store so I can get some makeup?"

Noah had said she didn't need makeup. He was correct; no one *needed* makeup. She loved makeup. She loved how she could change her look depending on her mood with makeup. She didn't need it, but she wanted it.

"Of course. You got everything you need?" Emory asked as they rifled through the cart full of clothes.

"Yeah." She headed toward the fitting room, but her mind was back at Moe's as she tried everything on to make sure it all fit properly. Only a few items went back to the rack. She would finally have some clothes that not only belonged to her but were her style. One more step to feeling like her old self again.

New clothes. A new job. And soon, makeup. Old Hollyn was emerging. And, depending on how the conversation went tonight, there might be a new and *improved* Hollyn bursting through the cocoon.

She preferred new and improved over scared and lost. That's how she'd felt the weeks she'd spent with Ravenwood. Although she knew they could protect her, she'd felt like she was watching someone's life play out on a movie screen, like a spectator in her own life. Since she'd pulled onto Noah's property, her heart and soul began to settle. Even before her magic had stretched toward Noah, she'd known she was where she was supposed to be, where she was supposed to stay.

The women helped her load her new clothes onto the counter. She ended up having fifty dollars of Noah's money left over. And she planned on paying him back for every penny as soon as she started working. Even if they decided to follow their other halves lead and bound themselves to each other, she never wanted to be dependent on another person.

What would he think when he saw her in clothes closer to her own style? Would he still find her attractive, or was he more into the country girl look? As comfortable as she felt in the middle of nowhere, she could never picture herself staying in flannels, t-shirts, and worn in jeans. It was cute on other women, just not her taste.

As she watched the pink, purple, and sparkly clothes bagged up, she couldn't help but get excited to work behind the bar again. She'd intentionally chosen clothes she knew would be eye catching, just like she'd always done. Yet, the only attention she found herself craving was from the big, burly, bearded Shifter.

She was a mess. Her mind was all over the place. Just like her emotions. Her magic had chosen Noah, but she still didn't like the thought of being bound for life to the same species that wanted to sell her and turn her into a slave.

Noah wasn't like that, though. She could feel it, deep down, even without her magic.

"You ready?" Emory asked as she grabbed a few bags.

"Someone better let me buy them something today," Nova said with a pout, little Rieka on her hip. Both children were so quiet and well-behaved. They'd barely made a peep since they left Blackwater territory.

Hollyn smiled as they headed to the parking lot, the women teasing back and forth. They were obviously close. And they'd welcomed Hollyn in with open arms in just one day. It had been so long since she'd been part of a family; it felt good.

The conversation tonight would determine whether she'd get to stay a part of the family or if she'd be all alone again. She knew they'd treat her well as long as she was there, but if Noah rejected what she had to tell him, she'd be on her own again, just like she'd been since she'd turned thirteen.

They headed to the drugstore, all the women and the two babies piling into the makeup aisle. Lola, Nova, and Shawnee had a blast perusing all the goodies while Emory and Peyton hung back and chuckled at their antics. Once Hollyn found the few things she needed – an eyeshadow palette, some liner, mascara, and gloss – they checked out and headed back for Blackwater.

"I'm not ready to go home. I'm getting cabin fever," Nova whined as they climbed into their cars.

"You're just mad no one let you buy a bunch of crap," Emory teased.

Nova, Peyton, and Callie turned off to where Emory said was Big River while Emory drove Shawnee and Hollyn back to Blackwater with Lola sitting in the back with little Grace. The conversation had waned, but mainly because the nerves were making Hollyn retreat into herself. She couldn't chat about makeup and clothes when she only had around seven hours before Noah would be home and they had a life changing moment.

"Thanks for today," Hollyn said to Emory.

"Anytime, Hollyn. Seriously. It's always nice to have more women around." She winked with a grin as Lola climbed into the front seat once Hollyn vacated it.

Hollyn lifted her hand as Emory backed the car out and disappeared around the corner. Shawnee helped Hollyn heft her bags inside.

"You know, when I first came here, Colton took me shopping. I only had a few changes of clothes that I hated," Shawnee said as they began to unbag the clothes and pop the tags so they could all be washed.

Hollyn moved Noah's clothes into the dryer. She'd fold them once they were done but wouldn't trespass into his room. Who knew how messy his bedroom would be?

"Why did you wear them if you hated them?" Hollyn asked, glancing over at her as she tossed a shirt into the washer.

Shawnee's narrow shoulders raised then fell. "Because I was supposed to. The females in my Pride are raised to be *pleasing and available*," she said, changing her tone to mock those last two words. "There was a certain image, a way we were to look, act, all that crap. I'm only with Colton because I was forced."

Anger bubbled up inside of Shawnee. Had she been wrong about these people? "Colton is forcing you to stay here?"

Shawnee looked up with wide eyes, holding her hands out in front of her. "No! Oh my gosh. I should've worded that differently. I was forced to find a mate or risk being sold off. Colton just happened to be looking for a mate, too. He's an old romantic and wanted a woman and cubs to dote on. It just turned out that we fell in love. Trust me when I say, my parents hate that I'm happy." The chuckle that escaped Shawnee was a mixture of sad and sarcastic.

"Your parents don't want you to be happy?" What kind of people raised a child to be miserable?

"I'm pretty sure they don't even know what happy is. They actually tried to take me away from Colton," Shawnee said, glancing at Hollyn from the corner of her eye, as if she wasn't sure whether she'd scare her away with the story.

"What happened?" Hollyn asked. They tossed the rest of the clothes in the wash then headed into the bathroom to put the rest of her makeup and toiletries away. Now that she stood in the bathroom and saw the shampoo and lone bar of soap sitting on the side of the tub, Hollyn wished she'd bought herself some body wash and maybe some decent shampoo and conditioner. Her hair would be in tangles after using the crap Noah had.

Shawnee leaned her hip against the vanity and tugged on a copper curl, wrapping it around her finger. It looked like a nervous habit, or maybe she was trying to find a way to avoid the story.

"You don't have to tell me," Hollyn said. The last thing she wanted was to make the small woman uncomfortable.

"No, it's not that I don't want to tell you. I just…I don't want to scare you off. That kind of stuff doesn't really happen. I mean, it does. But…shit," Shawnee said, tossing her hair over her shoulder. "I want you to stay here. I can tell you and Noah are clicking and I really want a sister-in-law."

Hollyn smiled despite herself. Her heart did a little squeeze at the thought of having a sister of any form. Even before she'd lost her parents, she'd always been an only child. No aunts. No uncles. So, no cousins, either.

"You won't scare me off," she said, and it was only a half lie. The part of her that was already tethered to Noah knew there was nothing that could make her leave. It was the part of her that made her run her whole life that told her this life, a life with Shifters, could be just as dangerous as it was on her own.

"Well, I told you my parents weren't thrilled that I was happy. It was more that they thought I should be with an Alpha. And they hated that I was working and making my own money. And that I no longer wore those stuffy clothes. And they were constantly on me about losing weight."

"What? You're gorgeous!" The woman had an hourglass figure and curves in all the right places.

"That's what Colton says," Shawnee said, averting her eyes as a pretty blush made her freckles pale. "Anyway," she said, waving off the compliment as if she were uncomfortable with it. "They showed up at Moe's one night and the bears and wolves from Big River ran them off. Then they showed up here when we were all asleep. The thing is, my lioness had been pretty submissive since I was a child." Shawnee explained how she'd had to train her lioness to stay away when she was being beaten as a child. She said it always got worse if her animal came forward to protect her.

"That's so messed up," Hollyn said with a sneer. Her own parents had always encouraged her to strengthen her gifts.

"Yeah. I know. So, they showed up and attacked. It was pretty scary. I thought I was going to lose Colton and the rest of the guys. Then Big River and a few other friends showed up. The Pride realized the fight was going to end badly for them. And then…my lioness got pissed and attacked. It was awesome." She grew a little breathless as her smile widened.

"I bet it was." Hollyn thought back to when her fire had come forth the first time. It was a rush she remembered over twenty years later.

"Why did you think you were going to lose Colton?"

"We were way outnumbered," Shawnee said, looking toward the door as if replaying the scene in her head. "There were over twenty lions and just the four bears. And me. But my lioness wouldn't come out at first. So…four bears against two dozen lions. They were all hurt pretty badly."

"They risked their lives for you?" Hollyn asked, once again awed at how close these people were. The more time she spent with them, the less they resembled the people she was taught to fear – for obvious reasons – and hid from for two decades.

"Of course they did. We're family."

There was that word again: Family. None of them were blood, but they'd grown their own families, built lives with each other and were more than happy to take a complete stranger out on the town and get her new clothes, just because they wanted her to feel like part of that family.

She just hoped Noah could accept her as easily as the women had.

****

Noah struggled to keep from shutting the bar down early. All he'd been able to think about all day was Hollyn, about the pull he felt toward her, and her promise to talk later. It was officially later.

"Time to go," Noah yelled the second the clock struck midnight.

"You didn't even warn last call," a Shifter complained as he tipped back his beer and finished it.

"You know what time I fucking close. Get your shit and get out," Noah yelled as he rushed to start his closing duties before the bar was even empty.

"What the hell is his problem tonight?" someone grumbled as they headed toward the door.

"Probably trying to get home to that little redhead he has working here," the first guy said with a chuckle. The sound made Noah want to throat punch the jackoff.

"That's Colton's mate, dumbass. Let's go," he yelled, making Shifters hustle a little faster out the door.

When the last person was gone, he locked the door and shut off the outside lights. He looked around. Fuck it. He could sweep and mop when he got in tomorrow morning. He wanted to get home. He wanted to see Hollyn. He wanted to find out what was going on between them, and he didn't mean in the chick flick kind of way. There was a physical thread tying them together and he wanted to find out what she'd meant about her magic being the cause.

She'd sworn she hadn't glamoured him, but there was a whole lot of shit at play. As much as he'd love to be paired with someone as hot as Hollyn, he refused to be forced into anything, and that counted by magic. Just because his bear had already chosen her didn't mean he had to listen.

His bear took the opportunity to chuckle a chuffing sound in Noah's head. Who was he fooling? His bear had chosen. It would be harder than fuck to ignore that kind of bond.

Jogging around the bar, Noah grabbed his keys, flipped off the lights inside, turned off the jukebox, then headed home. He normally kept the radio off during this drive; after hearing the jukebox and Shifters talking all day, he relished the silence.

Not tonight. He needed something to fill his thoughts other than Hollyn. Otherwise, he'd end up breaking the speed limit by a lot just to get back to her. He scanned through the stations until he found talk radio and tried to pay attention to what they were talking about.

Within ten minutes, his headlights flashed over his porch, and Hollyn was waiting out there, sitting on the top step with her arms wrapped around her knees.

She'd changed clothes. She was no longer wearing jeans that looked way too big for her or a t-shirt that hid those tits he'd fantasized about all day. Now, she was wearing a snug tank top and a pair of shorts.

It did nothing to help the need to touch her.

"Hey," he said as he climbed out of his truck. "You could've waited inside."

Did she think he didn't want her in his house when he wasn't home?

"It's too nice of a night to be inside." She tilted her head back and looked up at the sky. "You don't see that many stars where I lived." When she tilted her head back down, her eyes had faded to that amethyst color, but there was silver swirling within their depths. He couldn't wait to find out what the different colors meant. It was like her eyes were her own personal mood ring.

"Guess not," he said, lowering to sit on the step below her, putting him at eye level with her. She wasn't as petite as Shawnee and the other women in his life, but she was a lot smaller than his six foot seven.

They were quiet for a few heartbeats, just studying each other. He opened his mouth to break the silence but so did she.

“I wanted –"

“Did you –"

They laughed. Noah motioned for her to go first. It was like an awkward first date.

“You asked if I was glamouring you,” she said, turning her body so she was facing him.

He nodded and turned toward her, leaning one knee against the step she was sitting on.

“Okay,” she said, her eyes narrowed and darted away as she pulled her bottom lip between her teeth. Noah’s hand tingled to reach up and pull that lip free and run his fingertip over it to see if it was as pillowy soft as it looked.

“You know how you guys have animals inside of you and they just…pick your mate?”

“It’s not really that simple,” he said. She knew more about Shifters than he’d realized.

“It’s the closest thing I can think of for a comparison. So just roll with it. Okay,” she said, once again chewing on her bottom lip.

“You’ve got to stop doing that,” Noah blurted out and repositioned himself on the step as his jeans grew tighter.

“What?” she said with a frown.

He waved a finger at her mouth. “It just makes me want to kiss you.” Why did he say that? He shouldn’t have admitted that to her. Not yet.

Her frown deepened for a second then smoothed. A small smile tipped the corners of her lips and it sure as fuck looked like she liked the idea of his lips on hers, especially when her eyes dropped to his mouth for a brief second before raising to his face.

“What was I saying?”

He could see her as clearly in the dark as he could on a gray, cloudy day, and she was definitely flushed.

“Our animals choosing.”

"Right," she said, nodding her head quickly. "Right. Okay. So, you guys, Shifters, your animals pretty much tell you who your mate is. You form a bond with that person, even before you mark them."

"How the hell do you know so much about us?" Noah asked. There was no suspicion, just curiosity.

Hollyn's narrow shoulders rose and fell. "Fae are taught about any species that can be a danger to us. What I didn't learn from my parents, I learned from Aron and the other guys."

Noah grunted once and nodded for her to continue. He grunted instead of speaking because he didn't want her to hear the growl that was sure to come at the thought of Hollyn living with other men. Even if they were his friends and were just trying to protect her.

Hollyn's eyes roamed Noah's face for a brief second before she looked away, but it was enough for him to see yet another change to her eyes.

"Your eyes change colors like a Shifter," he said. She looked back at him with a confused look on her face. "I mean, they don't glow like ours, but they change colors."

"Yeah," she said on a sigh. "That happens sometimes. It makes it hard to be invisible around humans. Although, it usually only happens when I'm scared, angry or…"

"Or?" he asked when she didn't say anything else.

"Or my magic is trying to bind to someone."

Noah swallowed down another growl before speaking again. "It's happened before?"

"No."

One word. But it was beautiful.

"You were saying how you're kind of like Shifters when our animal chooses a mate."

"Right," she said, blinking rapidly as if she'd been zoned out. "When our magic finds its…how do I describe this? You know how magnets have a positive and negative? North and South?" Noah nodded. "My body is kind of a neutral where my magic acts as one side of a magnet. When it finds its other side, it begins to bind to it, whether I or the other party is interested in being with each other."

She was rambling, shaking her head like her own description wasn't what she'd wanted, how she'd wanted to explain it. "Okay. How about this, my magic has chosen you, and already began to bind us from the moment we met. We could go our own way, but we will both always feel this…pull, like we're tied together and straining against that rope. Does that make sense?"

He nodded slowly. He'd already begun to feel that. "Is there a way to break the bond?"

Disappointment flashed through her eyes and the amethyst slowly bled to a blue-gray color.

"I'm sure there is, but I don't know how."

She thought he wanted to break the bond. "How much do you know about the mating bond?" he asked, giving in to the temptation and raising his hand to brush the hair away from her face.

She leaned into his touch, nuzzling his hand for a second, and released a contented sigh.

Noah reluctantly pulled his hand away, but only because he wanted to have this conversation. And if he kept touching her, there was a good chance he'd scoop her in his arms, carry her to his bedroom, and plunge deep inside of her. That's not how he wanted his first time with her. Well, not true. He definitely wanted to feel her wrapped around him, but he wanted to take his time exploring her body and tasting every inch of her.

Hollyn frowned and pursed her lips in disappointment and Noah couldn't help but smile. He'd been in such a bad mood for the last few years, yet this woman was able to elicit a smile from him with a simple pout.

"So your magic is binding itself to me?" Noah asked, trying to get back to the conversation instead of focusing on how being near Hollyn made him feel lighter, happier, like he had the world sitting inches away from him.

Hollyn gave him a crooked grin. "Changing subjects?"

"I thought that was the subject," he teased, nudging her with his shoulder.

"I liked the subject of your hand on me."

And Noah had to once again adjust positions when his dick grew even harder, if that was at all possible.

Raising a brow at her, he waited for her to finish the story.

"Fine," she said, lifting a hand to push her hair behind her ear. "Yes. My magic started binding itself to you from the moment Aron pulled onto your territory. I tried to stop it. I'm not real hip on the whole not-choosing-for-myself thing. And I wasn't sure how you'd feel about being life and magic bound to a Fairy who might have Hell following behind. But…yeah. It's not permanent. Not yet."

"How does it become permanent?" Noah asked, his voice deeper from the lust and excitement over possibly having this incredible woman in his life.

Wait. Did he want to be bound for life? It was bad enough his animal declared her his mate without giving Noah the choice. But now Hollyn was telling him that they were fated rather than given a choice about their lives.

As he studied Hollyn, he watched in awe as her eyes flashed from sapphire to amethyst then back. Was she fighting the pull?

"Do you want this, Hollyn? Or is it like with Shifters?"

"What do you mean?" she asked, leaning back a little as her eyes bled back to sapphire and stayed that way for a few minutes.

"We don't really have much say in who our animals pick for us. I get that they have a more primal sense of our mates, that they can feel something we can't, but…do you have a choice? Do you want this? Do you want me or is it just your magic?"

For some reason, he couldn't fathom how a woman like Hollyn, someone so beautiful, so strong, so different from any woman he'd ever met would want to settle down with a bear Shifter who lived in the middle of nowhere and served beer in a hole-in-the-wall local bar. She was used to the city, used to bustling life, used to being surrounded by humans, not a bunch of raucous Shifters.

Hollyn's eyes narrowed and she seemed to be thinking about what he'd said. Finally, after a stretch of silence that had his nerves frayed, she shrugged slightly.

"I don't know."

Not quite the answer he'd wanted. Then again, he wasn't really sure what answer he wanted. Because, he wasn't sure how much of how he felt about Hollyn were his true feelings and how much was their supernatural DNA telling them how to feel.

Why the fuck couldn't his kind just find a woman they're interested in, fall in love, and decide whether or not they wanted to spend a lifetime together? Why did their animals get to choose?

He thought back on his last relationship; she was a prime example of why their human halves didn't choose their true mates. She was a waste of time and energy and just wanted a free ride. She was a compulsive liar and bordered on emotionally abusive. She'd also been the reason he'd stayed single for so long afterward.

His animal had tried to warn him, growling and snarling when they'd been together. He wasn't doing any of that now. With Hollyn so close, he sounded like a damn cat as he released a strange purring sound in Noah's head.

Around Hollyn, his bear was settled and content. Just like Noah.

"All I know is I feel safe around you," Hollyn said, snapping Noah's attention back to her. "That's something I haven't felt since I was a little girl. I know there are still risks, I know there are still people out there who'd love nothing more than to see how much money they could make from me. But with you, being near you, I feel like the rest of the world is so far away. Like...no one exists outside of this little bubble." She spun her index finger in a circle, indicating the territory.

Unfortunately, the world did still exist outside his territory. And, even if Aron and the rest of Ravenwood were able to locate and eliminate the current threat to Hollyn, there would always be others who would hunt her kind.

But he could keep her safe. He knew, without a doubt, he'd give his life for this woman. Mate or not, magic binding or not, he wanted her. He'd wanted her since he'd laid eyes on her this morning. Maybe they weren't in love, but he knew this woman would one day own his heart and soul like no one had in the past.

Chapter Five

Did she want this? That's what Noah had asked her. She'd thought about that very same question all day, but no matter how many different ways she tried to subdue her magic, no matter how many reasons she came up with as to why she shouldn't bind herself to a Shifter, she knew she was fighting a losing battle.

Noah was a good person. His people were good. Even before she'd found out they'd fought for the rights of female Shifters, she could tell they had good hearts. They'd welcomed her in with no questions, although other than Shawnee and Noah, they didn't really know how dangerous her presence could be to their existence. Shawnee had told her about the war they'd fought against her own family Pride, how she'd thought she'd lose the entire Clan. Would they want another fight? Would they want to go through all that again because of her?

Noah was watching her closely, his eyes slowly roaming her face as if memorizing it. She couldn't say she loved this man, but there were a lot of emotions she couldn't quite identify. There was a ton of lust, no doubt about that. He was gorgeous. So big and thick and scruffy.

She'd never been into scruffy guys, had never been one of those women who got hot over beards. But Noah wore it well. Even the t-shirt he wore made her all tingly the way it stretched across his broad chest and muscular arms. She knew he could protect her. And she'd protect him.

She'd given him a tiny demonstration of her gift earlier in the day. What would he do if he knew how powerful her Elemental gifts were? Would it scare him? Nah. Noah didn't seem like the kind of person who'd be scared by much.

As they sat silently regarding each other, she felt the tendrils of her magic reaching for him, begging her to finish the binding so it could wrap itself fully around Noah. To embed itself in every cell of Noah's body.

"There's more," she said, closing her eyes and digging deep for the courage she needed to warn Noah of their future.

"More what?" he asked. Ooooh. His voice was deep and growly and she had to clench her thighs against the sensation his voice sent through her body. *Focus, dammit.*

"More to the story."

Noah turned more toward her and leaned his back against the railing. He nodded once, his eyes never leaving her face.

"Soooo." It was bad enough that he obviously didn't like the fact that neither of them really had a choice in their relationships. She could only imagine how he'd react to the rest of it. "Remember how I told you my magic was trying to bind to you? That it wasn't permanent yet and all that?" He nodded once again. "Once the binding is finished, once we're bound for life…you'll have a piece of my magic inside of you."

His eyes narrowed and his brows lowered, only one side of his face was lit by the windows behind them. "I don't know what that means."

"You know how kids will cut their hands and press them together to be blood brothers or blood sisters? You know how we all thought it meant we'd carry a piece of each other with us?"

"I've never done that," he said, wrinkling his nose in a boyishly cute manner.

"You know what I'm talking about, though."

"I guess."

"What it means is, if we complete the binding, my magic will tether itself to you. It'll flow through your veins, almost as powerfully as it does mine."

His brows flew up and his eyes widened. "If I'm bound to you, I'll become a fucking Fairy?"

"What?" she said and released a loud, surprised laugh. "Oh my gosh. No. You're either born a Fairy or you're not, Noah. We can't change someone like Shifters can." She giggled as she tried to picture Noah resembling the Fae of her parents' time, back when their hair was almost as fair as their skin. "I mean, you'll have my magic flowing through your veins. You'll be able to feel me, feel my presence, and even my emotions, no matter how far away you are."

Noah sat staring at Hollyn, chewing on the newest information she'd dumped on him.

And then a slow, wide smile stretched across his face. "I'd be able to find you anywhere," he said, rather than asked.

"Yeah. But you'd also be able to feel any pain I go through, any sadness. It can be overwhelming for a non-Fae."

"But I'd be able to find you, no matter where you are. No matter how far away you are."

She lifted her shoulders in a slight shrug. "Yeah."

"How do we complete the bond?" Noah asked, standing and pulling her to her feet with his hand wrapped around hers.

"Noah," she said, tugging on her hand to try to pull him to a stop. Damn, the man was strong. He wasn't hurting her, wasn't holding her hand in a death grip, but her feet were almost sliding on the wood deck as she tried to pull back, tried to stop him from rushing into this. "Listen to me."

He glanced back at her, saw the fear and trepidation in her ever-changing eyes, and slowed to a stop just as he wrapped his big hand around the doorknob. Releasing his hold on her hand, his eyes darted to it. "Did I hurt you?" he asked, his eyes taking on a faint glow.

"No, of course not." And she had zero fear that he would, either. "I just want you to think about what you're asking. Are we sure we want to do this? We've known each other one day, Noah. You know nothing about me. I know nothing about you. Other than you're a Shifter who owns a bar and lives like a pig." She winked to soften her last words. Even if they were the truth.

He blinked. Then blinked again. Then he dropped his head and put his hands on his hips. "What the fuck am I doing?" he muttered to himself. After a few seconds, he lifted his head and frowned hard at the cabin next door. "Let's go in the house."

"Noah—"

"Shawnee's over there cheering us on. She's listening to every single word." He glared at the house as if he could see the redhead.

Hollyn just smiled. Shawnee hadn't made it a secret that she wanted to see Noah settled down. With a soft chuckle, she followed

Noah into the house and sat on the couch as he closed the door then ran a rough hand through his hair.

That same hand dragged down his face, weariness finally evident in their brown depths now that she could see him in the brightly lit living room.

"You might not be glamouring me, but I feel so fucking weird around you. Like I'm in a dream and have no control over my own damn actions." He paced from one end of the living room to the other.

"That's what I'm trying to warn you, Noah. It'll only get worse if we close the bond. What are you going to do if you're at work and I fall and hurt myself? You'll feel my pain, Noah. You'll worry. I've seen non-Fae go insane because of the bond."

She hated having to tell him all of this. It would've been so much easier if she'd just let things proceed naturally, just let her magic have its way. But she couldn't do that to him. She wanted him to have every single fact up front.

But when he turned to her, his eyes blazing bright, she wondered if her earlier feelings of safety were wrong. He looked terrifying as his lip pulled back in a snarl.

"I need to Shift," he growled out.

Hollyn swallowed hard and nodded. She couldn't seem to force her voice out through her tightening throat. Had she pissed him off? Had she been wrong about his character and his heart?

No way. Even if her brain refused to acknowledge red flags, her magic had never let her down. Except when it allowed her to be drugged and kidnapped.

But had that been a failure of her magic, or had it known her fate long before she had? If that asshole hadn't stuck her with a syringe, hadn't dragged her into the woods of Kansas City, Aron never would've found her. And he never would've brought her to the bears of Blackwater.

And she never would've met Noah.

Noah's movements were jerky as he walked toward the door, pulling at the back collar of his shirt and yanking it over his head. And her mouth went dry. If she'd thought he was hot clothed, it was nothing compared to Noah shirtless. The muscles in his back and shoulder rippled with each movement.

Hollyn averted her eyes as he opened the door and shoved his jeans over his hips until they were pooled at his feet. She glanced up just as he pulled the door shut and got an eyeful of a very impressive package. Magic or not, Noah was one hell of a specimen of the male species.

Before the door was fully closed, Hollyn heard several pops. Noah grunted.

Then a loud thud hit the front porch and shook the windows. Hollyn leapt from the couch and ran to the window, barely catching a glimpse of fur as Noah's bear took off for the woods across from the cabin.

And then Hollyn was alone again.

She stood at the door and watched for more movement, but her eyes weren't as sensitive as a Shifter's. Noah could be standing within the tree line looking right at her and she'd never know it.

Which sent fear slithering through her for other reasons. Someone could be right outside the house and Hollyn wouldn't know it. They could've been watching her sitting on the porch alone while she waited for Noah to get home and she'd have been none the wiser.

Just because her magic let her know when someone had a dark heart didn't mean she was warned of someone's presence, not until they were close enough.

Reaching forward, she turned the lock on the door and backed away from the windows. The thought of being watched gave her the damn creeps.

Hollyn lowered onto the couch and wrapped her arms around herself. Now that Noah had Shifted and charged into the woods, she wasn't sure what to do. She had no idea whether there was another room where she could sleep or if she was crashing on his couch for the time it took Aron to end the threat.

And she had no idea whether her admission to Noah had completely ruined her chance at happiness or not. She had no idea what had made him need to Shift, need to run, need distance from her. He must've felt secure enough that his Clan family would hear if there was any danger for him to leave her alone again.

Or maybe he realized he no longer cared enough. For some reason, that thought cut her deeply.

Leaning to the side, Hollyn lowered onto the couch, keeping her arms wrapped around her for warmth. He didn't even have a blanket on the couch to wrap herself in. But he had left his shirt.

Sitting up quickly, she shuffled to where he'd dropped his clothes, folded his jeans and laid them over the back of the couch before pulling on his large shirt. The hem fell past her knees. It was still warm from his body and smelled strongly of his scent. It was spicy and heady and pure masculinity.

Heading back to the sofa, she pulled her arms through the sleeves and used the shirt as a make shift sleeping bag. Closing her eyes, she let images of Noah, the sensation of his warm hand on her cheek lull her into a restless, nightmare filled sleep.

And then the nightmares just…stopped. She was filled with so much peace and warmth. She was floating. No. Something solid was against her, strong arms surrounded her. Forcing her lids open, she blinked up at Noah's face. He was carrying her. Where? Where the hell was she?

Noah's cabin. She'd fallen asleep after he'd left. What time was it? How long had he been gone? She was too tired to voice any of those questions, though. She just let Noah carry her until he gently lowered her onto a bed that smelled like him.

Pulling the blankets over her, he stood there, staring down at her before turning and leaving the room, pulling the door behind him while leaving it open enough she could see light coming from somewhere down the hall.

She smiled sleepily then let her body sink into the soft mattress below her. This time, when she fell asleep, she didn't have a single dream. Just peaceful, restful sleep. Something she hadn't experienced in months.

When Hollyn woke again, there was a sliver of hazy sunlight shining through the gap in the curtains. They were pulled closed, but the fabric didn't meet each other, allowing enough light into the room for Hollyn to avoid disorientation.

She was alone in the bed. Where was Noah? Not beside her in the bed where he'd laid her after roaming the woods. Not on the floor, either. Climbing from the bed, she tiptoed to the door and heard a deep, rumbling snore. Following the sound, she smiled down at Noah's big body squished up on the couch. Poor thing was way too big for the small piece of furniture. It would've been the right size for her. Why hadn't he just left her where she'd slept and gone to bed?

Looking around, she wasn't sure what she should do while she waited. One thing she knew she needed was a shower. And she'd get to wear some of her new clothes. What time did Noah need to be up? What time would he leave for work? Surely, he had some kind of alarm set for the day. It was Sunday, so maybe the bar didn't open as early as the rest of the week.

As quietly as possible, she grabbed some of her new clothes and the bag of makeup, cringing when the plastic bag it came in crinkled, and hurried to the bathroom. Once she was showered, she left her black hair to dry on its own and focused on applying eye makeup. After a swipe of gloss, she smiled at her reflection.

"Hello, old friend," she whispered. But her smile began to falter as she looked down at the purple, sleeveless top. She couldn't wait to get out of the flannels, but in these clothes, she felt like an imposter.

Perhaps it wasn't the clothes and makeup making her feel as if she were living someone else's life, but the fact she once again felt herself trying to slide into anonymity. Even without talking to Noah, she was prepared to call Aron, prepared to tell him this situation wouldn't work out and she needed to go somewhere else.

Could she, though? Even without the bond completed, could she just walk away from Noah and be happy ever again? Or would she be leaving a piece of herself, a piece of her heart and soul with him?

Hollyn pulled the door open and peeked her head out. That slow, steady snore still filled the room. Poor guy was probably exhausted after being woken up so early yesterday, working all day, then running the woods, clearly to get some space between them.

In her bare feet, she padded over to the couch and looked down at him. One arm was thrown over his eyes, the other rested on his stomach. And the only thing hiding his junk was a throw pillow.

Whoa. Did that mean he'd carried her to the bedroom naked last night? He'd had her up against his body when there was a definite attraction between them, regardless of Shifter or Fae bond, and he hadn't tried a thing. At least she didn't remember him trying anything.

No way. Noah wasn't like that. Besides, she'd have remembered if someone like him had touched her. She'd have woken up moaning and begging for more.

Stepping away, she dug deep to see how much of what she was thinking at that moment was her magic and how much was just her.

It was all her. Her magic recognized Noah for what he would be to them in the future. But her heart and body were his, even without the damn bond.

****

Noah groaned as he rolled over. Why the hell hadn't he gotten a big ass couch like Colton? Oh. That's right. Because he was never home enough to enjoy it. He'd had no idea he'd ever sleep on the fucking thing.

Every muscle ached as he pushed to a sitting position. A glance at his phone elicited a slew of curses. The last thing he wanted to do was go into work. He wanted to stay here and talk to Hollyn.

When she'd told him that her magic would embed itself inside of him if they'd completed the bond, that he'd feel her no matter where she was, he'd felt as if someone possessed him and he was ready to run inside and do whatever was necessary.

Luckily, Hollyn had kept her wits about her. Then Shawnee stood inside the cabin she shared with Colton and cheered him on, told him that Hollyn was made for him, that they would make the perfect couple. He was pretty sure she'd say that about any female he brought home. Not that he'd brought Hollyn home.

Nope. She'd been delivered straight to his door like a gift.

The more Hollyn explained, the more his beast tried to burst through to mark her. He didn't give a fuck what tying them to Hollyn would mean; he just wanted their mate. So, Noah had given his body to his bear and run the woods for hours, always staying close enough to scent anyone who might creep up on the property and to hear Hollyn if she needed him.

When he'd returned, she'd been out cold on the couch. And she'd been wearing his shirt. A rush of masculine pride rushed through him until he realized it was because she was cold. He didn't have blankets or any of that crap like Shawnee had bought for Colton's. She'd just pulled it on and made herself as small as possible to cover what parts of her body she could.

This strange sensation squeezed his heart as he'd watched her sleep. No way was her magic at play. And his bear was quiet since he'd let him run the forest. No. This was pure affection for the beautiful raven-haired, sapphire-eyed woman who looked like she was having a nightmare.

Noah had scooped her into his arms as gently as possible and carried her to his only bed. He had a two-bedroom cabin, just like the rest of the guys, but he'd never had the time to furnish it any further than what he needed to be comfortable. Now, he wished he'd had a second bed. And a bigger couch. And maybe cleaned up a little.

He took the time to check his place out as he carried her across the room; she and Shawnee had definitely put in some work. His house looked great. They cleared the sink, picked up all his dirty clothes and threw out the empty pizza boxes. They must think he was lazy. No. Shawnee knew better. She knew he was never home. And since Hollyn worked the same kind of job her whole life, she knew how tiring it was to come home so late and have zero energy or desire to clean.

Noah had pushed his door open with his toe and glanced down at Hollyn in time to see her lids flutter a few times, open, then close again. Her muscles had relaxed in his hold, the crease between her brows smoothed. He'd chased away her nightmares. Or he'd hoped.

As he scrubbed his hands over his face, he couldn't help but remember the way she'd felt pressed up against him, the way her body felt in his arms, the soft sigh she'd released when he'd covered her up.

His dick thumped against the pillow he'd covered up with before passing out last night.

He needed a cold shower and some coffee before Hollyn found him out there naked. Tossing the pillow aside, he stood, pulling his arms over his head, stretched and grimaced at all the pops. He wasn't far from forty, but his body felt way older than it was. He needed a break. Bad. Hell; he needed a full vacation.

Noah turned to head for the shower and froze, his eyes going wide. Just like Hollyn's.

She stood outside the front door, her hand frozen on the knob. Her gaze went from his eyes and made a slow path down his body, lingering on his dick before jerking back to his face. Her cheeks flushed a bright pink before she turned quickly.

"I'm sorry," she said, her voice slightly muffled through the door.

"Fuck." Noah hurried through the house to his bedroom. He yanked on a pair of sweats and pulled a t-shirt over his head. It did nothing for the instant boner he got from her slow perusal of his body. She'd looked like she'd liked what she'd seen, at least until she realized she was staring at him naked.

Noah put his hand on the door knob and took a few breaths, bringing every unsexy thing he could to mind to kill his hard on. When he was ready, he pulled the door open and sought out Hollyn. She was sitting on the front porch, her back to him, her arms wrapped around her knees the way she'd been last night when he got home from work.

After another deep breath, he stepped out onto the porch. "Hey," he said, his voice still hoarse from sleep.

"Hey," she said, looking at him over her shoulder. "I promise I didn't do that on purpose," she said. Her cheeks were still pink but there was a smile on her lips now. "Although, I'm not exactly disappointed."

Aaaand his dick grew again. "Tease," he said, pulling the door shut and moving toward her. He held his hand out to her and pulled her to her feet. "Don't feel like listening to Shawnee." He jerked his head toward her house.

She hadn't paid much attention to the two of them outside yet, probably because she was getting ready for work, but it was just a matter of time.

Hollyn slipped her small, cool hand into his and let him hoist her to her feet. She kept her hand in his as they went back inside. That was fine with him. He loved the feeling of any part of her in his hands.

She let Noah guide her into the house. He lifted her hand and kissed the back of it before releasing it.

"You're not scared of much, are you?" he said as he jerked his head toward the kitchen table as he headed into the kitchen to make coffee.

"Seriously? I'm terrified of everything," she said, her voice an octave higher.

He turned and looked at her over his shoulder before turning back around and pouring water into the tank. Once the amber liquid was running into the carafe, he turned and leaned against the cabinet with his hands on the counter behind him.

She sure as hell didn't act scared. And definitely not terrified. When she'd first arrived yesterday, he'd felt her nerves rolling from her, but why wouldn't she be nervous? She'd been rescued from a trafficker and dumped off at some stranger's house. Not just any stranger, but a Shifter, someone she was taught to fear.

His little Fae was strong. Stronger than anyone he'd ever met. Not only did she not show any fear, but she was willing to tie herself to him, to a Shifter, to someone she was supposed to run from, for the rest of her life.

But why?

He understood the bond. He understood how he felt now that his animal had pretty much claimed her. If she left, if she decided this life wasn't for her, he'd grieve her loss for the rest of his life. Even if he dated, he'd always feel empty, hollow, as if a piece of his soul had been torn away.

Hollyn's bond, her *magic's* bond, was more complex. While he couldn't really mark her for fear of poisoning her or turning her he had no idea whether a Fairy could even be turned – she could bind them, which would mean a piece of her magic would stay inside of him permanently. As freaked out as he was by that thought, his bear loved the idea of being able to find her.

If any fucker ever got his hands on her again, he'd know where she was and be able to get to her side before anything could happen to her. But he'd also feel her emotions, feel her pain, as she would his.

The pros far outweighed the cons.

"Do you think this is all weird?" she asked, snapping him out of his back and forth in his mind.

"Which part? The fact I turn into a big bear or the fact you're a real life Fairy who can conjure fire with your hands?" he teased, pouring them both coffee and carrying it over to the table.

"No," she said on a chuckle. She smiled up at him as she took the mug. "The fact we talked about being bonded for life and we haven't even kissed yet."

And now all he wanted to do was kiss her. Not yet. Not until after he'd showered and brushed his teeth. He probably smelled like a mixture of fur, forest, and sweat. Not to mention the morning breath.

"You saying you want me to kiss you?" he said, then winked at her when her cheeks went pink again.

"I want more than a kiss," she mumbled under her breath. Surely, she had to know he'd heard her clearly. But she didn't look embarrassed, didn't look up at him with wide eyes. If he didn't see her naked soon, he would end up with a permanent case of blue balls with as often as he'd been hard in the last twenty-four hours.

He had to change the subject and fast. "I have to go to work soon. You still want to tend bar?"

Her face brightened and he realized she was wearing makeup. Not too much. She was pretty either way, but the makeup really brought out those gorgeous, unique eyes of hers. "Absolutely. I mean, the girls think it's safe. And you'll be there." Her features darkened with anger. "And no asshole will sneak up on me this time. Anyone tries anything, they're getting fried."

She lifted her hand and a ball of fire danced in her palm.

"I know that should make me nervous, and you're going to think I'm nuts…but that is such a turn on."

"Really?" she said, closing her hand around the flame with a teasing smile.

He pointed to his crotch hidden behind the table. She didn't stand up and come to inspect it, but she did sit up a little more and crane her neck as if trying to see under the table. She then sat back and winked. "Just kidding."

"I wasn't," he said behind his mug as he went to take a sip.

"Is what I'm wearing okay for work?" she asked, smoothing her hand down her top and Noah's eyes followed that movement. He never thought he'd be jealous of someone's own hands in his life.

"You look fine," he said and cleared his throat. Not that it would help the deep growly sound caused by lust. "I've got to shower. Help yourself to the fridge or you can wait to eat at the bar."

"Won't I be too busy to eat at work?"

"It's Sunday. We're usually pretty slow on Sundays."

Noah pushed to his feet and shuffled down the hall, snagging his phone from the couch as he passed. He wasn't looking forward to the tantrum Shawnee would throw when he told her he didn't need her to come in today. He didn't need them both there on the slowest day of the week.

Shawnee surprised him when she sent a lone heart emoji in response. Guess Colton convinced her they could spend some alone time since she was off for the day.

Hurrying through his shower, he brushed his teeth, combed his beard, then used his fingers to comb his hair. He kept it short purposely so he wouldn't have to mess with it every day. It was just one more thing that would cost him precious minutes that he didn't have to spare.

Noah wrapped the towel around his waist and hurried to his bedroom where he pulled on a pair of jeans and t-shirt, then grabbed his socks and headed into the living room. Hollyn was still sitting at the table, but she'd turned the chair toward the room and pulled her feet into a criss-cross position. "How're the fire codes in this area?" she asked.

Noah frowned at her as he lowered onto the couch to pull on his boots. "What do you mean?"

"I do this fire breathing trick. Humans think I'm blowing burning alcohol, although I'd still want the Shifters to think that's all it was, too."

Even after spending the whole day with his friends and after telling him about her magic trying to bind them, she was still nervous about other Shifters finding out what she was. Although, it was probably safer if they didn't know. Just because his people would never turn her over didn't mean there weren't assholes who came into his place who wouldn't jump on the first opportunity to make a buck.

"Do any humans go to your place?" Hollyn asked, finally dropping her legs and grabbing a pair of tennis shoes and slipping them on.

"Occasionally. That's how Peyton and Tristan met."

"Peyton is the blonde Nova calls Cujo, right?" she asked, standing and sliding her hands into her back pockets. The motion pushed her chest out and drew Noah's gaze directly to them.

"Yeah," Noah said, dragging his gaze back up to her face. "Tristan is a wolf from Big River. They'll eventually come into the bar for lunch. And Nova likes to have all these cookouts. You'll meet all the guys eventually."

He watched her eye color change, but it wasn't dramatic. And the scent rolling from her was more anxiety than fear. Good. Because he really wanted her to like his friends.

"You ready?"

"Yep," she said, following him through the door.

As she followed close behind, all Noah could think about was their earlier conversation about her wanting him to kiss her, about wanting more than just a kiss. He was so tempted to turn and press his lips to hers, but wasn't sure how she'd react to that. And he wasn't sure he wanted to risk binding them even further.

And since she hadn't brought it up again, he figured he'd let her lead. In the meantime, he'd have to do everything in his power to avoid touching her. And he had to keep his bear under control when other males talked to her and flirted with her while she was making drinks.

This was going to be a long fucking day.

Chapter Six

Just as he feared, the second word got out that Noah had hired a new woman to work behind the bar, the place began to fill up. Pulling his phone from his pocket, he apologized and then begged Shawnee to come in, even offering to keep a beer in front of Colton at all times, on Noah's dime.

Fifteen minutes later, a beaming Shawnee showed up, Colton, Luke, Carter, Gray, Reed, Tristan, Micah, and all the women in tow, minus the babies.

"I asked her to come in because we were slammed. Why the hell did you invite everyone else?" Noah chided Colton.

"I just mentioned to Carter we were coming up. You can blame him for this," Colton said, waving toward the entirety of Blackwater and Big River.

Noah turned his glare on Carter. There was no humor, no apologetic smile. He just kept looking from Noah to Hollyn and back again. He wanted an explanation. He'd barely told Carter Hollyn was staying at his house and that Aron had dropped her off. He'd yet to tell him everything. He wasn't happy.

With a nod, he silently promised his stand-in Alpha – bear Shifter Clans didn't have Alphas – that he'd fill him in on everything. Just not now. Now, he had a bar full of Shifters watching Hollyn.

Hollyn filled the drinks as fast as they came in, tossing a bottle behind her back and flipping it in her hand. She poured interesting cocktails when someone would tell her to make whatever she wanted.

Looking around the room, he suppressed the growl at so many sets of eyes glued to Hollyn. His anger and possessiveness were twofold – she was supposed to be hidden away, away from Shifters who could possibly tell others of her presence. That was a huge part of why he hadn't yet told any of his Clan or his friends what she was.

The other and biggest part was the way his bear begged to be released. Too many males were watching her, smiling at her, flirting with her.

Mine, his bear growled in his head.

Yeah. I feel ya.

Shawnee smiled and laughed as she carried orders to the tables. Hollyn had the drinks under control, and no one was ordering food. Noah didn't have shit to do.

So, he did something he'd wanted to do for years instead of Shifting his teeth and snapping at every fucker who dared look in Hollyn's direction – he rounded the bar and sat with his friends. Leaning back, he watched Hollyn's performance. He couldn't help the rush of pride at how skilled she was, at how entertaining she was behind the bar.

Her eyes lifted and met his. Her smile widened and two things happened: his heart tripled its pace and his animal roared its approval inside his head. Noah was lost in her eyes. Lost in Hollyn. He knew it didn't matter how hard both of them fought against fate or whatever it was pushing them together; they were meant to be in each other's lives. He knew, deep down in his heart, he'd been born to take care of Hollyn, to make her happy, to make her smile. Just like she'd been born to melt his icy heart.

The jukebox was blaring Chris Stapleton music, but it was barely heard over the crowd as Hollyn locked eyes with him, shrugging as she stepped onto the bar. Oh shit. Was she going to…

Hollyn put a bottle to her lips and pretended to take a long pull. She then lit a match and blew a ball of flames. Even from halfway across the room, Noah could feel the heat.

Her show was probably *really* against the fire code, but he didn't see any fire fighters or the fire Chief anywhere. It was his bar. As long as she didn't burn the place down, he'd sit back and let her perform.

As much as he loved the idea of the bar being far in the black and the girls' pockets being full of tips, he loved the joy shining bright on Hollyn's face even more. She was doing something she loved, something she was good at. It was part of her old life that she'd gotten back. He loved watching her like that, loved the smile that stayed permanently on her face.

And…he loved her. Two days and he could feel his heart swell for her. His beast already claimed her. He could never mark her, but he could let Hollyn bind them with her magic. That was enough for him. Hell, just her saying she'd stay with him would be enough. As long as he had her in his life.

He'd do anything to keep her safe. He'd protect her with his own fucking body if he had to. And he knew his friends would keep her safe, too. He knew they'd watch over her just like the bears helped to watch over their mates and cubs.

He knew he loved her, but Hollyn had been right about something; they knew nothing about each other. He still had no idea whether she had a family looking for her. Friends? If her former boss noticed she was gone, he either reported it to the human cops, who couldn't do a damn thing, or he thought she'd just quit and didn't give a shit.

There was more, too. He wanted to know everything. He wanted to know her favorite color and favorite food, her favorite music and movies. He wanted to know all her deep, dark secrets. And he wanted her to know his life, too. Not that he had any secrets. After his parents had died, he'd pretty much just worked nonstop, stepping in to fight beside his friends when they needed him.

"She's really good," Emory yelled over the noise.

Noah nodded with a grunt, but he didn't look away from the beautiful woman stacking shot glasses for another trick. His face split with a grin as she did this thing where she held up the shakers and poured shots evenly, but the colors changed for each shot.

And then she looked up to see if he was watching. He gave her a wink and a nodded of approval. What he really wanted to do was take her home, pour those shots all over her body, and lick them off.

"So you two gonna date or what?" Nova yelled over the chatter and music.

Noah looked around to see if anyone was paying attention. "What are you talking about?" Just because Hollyn and Noah were talking about it didn't mean he wanted the whole world to know yet. He still had to talk to Carter and the rest of the Clan. But honestly, if they thought her presence was too dangerous, Noah knew he'd leave with her. It didn't matter to him that it was happening too soon or that he'd feel her emotions; Hollyn was his.

“You have goo goo eyes,” Nova said, propping her chin in her hand and batting her lashes.

“What the hell are goo goo eyes?” Noah grumbled, finally peeling his stare from Hollyn to frown at Nova.

She waved a hand around Noah’s face and raised her brows as if that explained everything.

Turning to Gray, he shook his head. “Does she ever exhaust you?”

Gray snorted and grinned. “Every day, man.”

“Hey!” Nova said, sitting up and jabbing her elbow into Gray’s ribs.

“She’s trying to say you two look like you’re in love,” Callie said from beside Micah whose arm was draped possessively around her shoulders. His coyote-wolf mix didn’t like so many males around their mate. Micah had always had a hard time controlling his animal half.

Noah had never understood that. Until yesterday. His bear was constantly scratching at his skin to get out. But he couldn’t mark Hollyn. It was like he was constantly repeating that to himself and his bear for fear his animal would force a change and hurt the Fairy who was currently laughing as some dickhead leaned over the bar and said something to her.

Her smile faltered a bit and the humor left her eyes. She glanced in his direction then back at the guy. Even from where he sat, he could see her tense as the smile completely faded from her face and she shook her head a couple of times and took a step back. When the fucker leaned forward, his hand outstretched, Noah realized he had two choices: Get his ass up and stop the dick wad or let his bear have his skin.

Shifting in his own bar was out of the question. He’d told every single Shifter who’d come in to stay human more than once. He couldn’t go against his own rule.

Run the asshole off it was, then.

Pushing to his feet, Noah kept his focus on Hollyn, internally warning her to keep her gifts to herself. She didn’t need them to feel safe, not here, not with Noah, the rest of Blackwater, and all of Big River there. If she conjured any fire, everyone would know she wasn’t just some human woman he’d hired. They’d know immediately she was an Elemental Fairy. And just because he trusted his friends, didn't mean he trusted anyone else there. Even the best people could be turned bad for the right amount of money.

Noah rounded the bar and stood in front of Hollyn, crossing his thick arms over his chest. "You need something?" he asked.

The male's eyes left Hollyn and lifted to Noah. The dude was a Shifter, but he was smaller than Noah, thinner. "Was just trying to get that pretty thing to go out with me," the dude slurred.

"Looks like she's not interested." Noah said, turning to glance at Hollyn over his shoulder as if confirming his statement. She mimicked Noah's stance with her arms crossed and her feet spread hip width apart. She shook her head. "There you go. She's not interested. Go find your friends. Leave her the fuck alone or get the fuck out."

The guy was drunk, but he didn't appear to have a clue about Hollyn's bloodline, nor did he appear dangerous. Just horny and intoxicated – never a good mix.

"I didn't know she was taken. Sorry," the guy said, holding his hands up and turning to walk away. He snapped his fingers and turned back. "Forgot my drink. You're a lucky bastard. Hope you know that. Not many humans can handle this shit, and you've got one who obviously can."

The fact he was talking about dating human women made Noah a little uneasy; it would take one bad date for his entire species to be exposed. But Noah relaxed and shook his head when the guy saluted him with his glass, sloshing alcohol everywhere.

Turning to check on Hollyn, his breath caught in his lungs when she grabbed his face, pulled him down, and pressed her lips to his. She held there for a few breaths until her body began to mold against his and her arms wrapped around his neck. Noah pulled her closer, tangling one hand in her hair and tilted her head to deepen the kiss. She'd drank something sweet. Her lips were softer than he could've imagined. And if there had been even a sliver of doubt that Hollyn was his, that doubt was erased by the feel of her in his arms. It was perfect. She was perfect. The moment for their first kiss might've been far from perfect, but he had a feeling he knew why she did it; she was letting the entire room know her heart was claimed.

****

If Hollyn could've climbed Noah's body, she would have. But there was a roomful of people watching their PDA. Not that she cared if they saw her kissing Noah. She was done fighting it. She was done trying to resist the urge to feel him against her. Even if they didn't close the bond soon, she needed to feel Noah inside of her. And she gave zero shits that it had only been two days. They'd just pretend it had been two dates. So what if it was one day short of the unspoken rule of waiting three dates.

Pulling from Noah, she giggled at the rattling feeling under her palm as he growled his disappointment. Yep. She felt the same way. But they couldn't exactly get naked and bump uglies on the bar top.

Noah bent and pressed one more kiss to her lips, then the tip of her nose, then her forehead where he lingered, his breath warming her face. He was so big and kind of burly, and now she was seeing a more affectionate, sweeter side of him. She had to admit, she liked both sides. And she really wanted to see his bear. She'd only caught a glimpse of him last night, but she wanted to see him face to face, feel his fur, look into his animal's eyes.

Would his bear recognize her? She had some questions for Noah, questions she hadn't bothered to ask Aron because she frankly never thought she'd need to know.

Noah took a step back and bent his knees so they would be closer to eye to eye. "You okay or do you want me to take over?"

"I'm good," she said and realized how breathless she sounded. One kiss and she was about to have a heart attack. She could imagine how her body would react once they were finally naked.

As much fun as she was having, she couldn't wait for the night to end.

And in a blink of an eye, it did. Noah came back around the bar and helped her wash dishes. "Last call, assholes," he bellowed out.

Hollyn turned wide eyes on him. "You always talk to your customers like that?"

He frowned at her in confusion. "Like what?"

"You just called everyone assholes."

Noah straightened and looked around. "Well…they are. Most of them, anyway."

"I don't think they even notice," Shawnee said as she brought more empty glasses to them and tossed the empty bottles.

Noah's friends called their goodnights, told her how awesome she was and how much they couldn't wait to see more. And then it was just Shawnee, Colton, Noah, and Hollyn.

Colton helped Shawnee stack the chairs while she swept up dirt and broken glass. Hollyn and Noah worked behind the bar, restocking and cleaning the glasses.

"You guys want us to stick around?" Colton asked through a yawn when Shawnee was done with her closing duties.

"Nah. We're good. Thanks. Go home. I'll talk to you tomorrow," Noah said, waving them off.

As Noah followed them so he could lock the door behind them, Hollyn continued with the closing duties, dancing to Bon Jovi's *You Give Love a Bad Name*. When Noah caught her, she made her moves bigger, pretending she was in the video, even using a beer bottle as a microphone. She swung her head, making her hair go everywhere until Noah was laughing.

He had no idea how big of a dork she could be at times, but she had a feeling after meeting all of his friends, he was fine with that. They'd been so funny and treated her as if she'd been one of them for years.

Noah's hand lowered and he rearranged his junk. A rather impressive bulge made her swallow hard. She remembered how he'd looked naked. And couldn't wait to see all of him again.

The music changed to Two Feet's *I Feel Like I'm Drowning*. Hollyn decided to use the music and her love of dance to her advantage. Noah seemed like the kind of guy who would wait for her to make the move for fear of making her feel rushed. So, she'd just show him exactly what she wanted.

Coming around the bar, she used the bar stools, the tables, anything she could as a prop, spinning, opening her legs, swinging her hips, even turning and bending so he got a good look at her butt as she stood slowly, running her hands up the back of her thighs.

Before the song was over, Noah took three long strides in her direction and tangled his hands in her hair, tilting her head back and crashing his lips over hers. There was nothing hesitant or unsure about this kiss. It was full of need and lust and want. His tongue danced in her mouth, moving with the same sensuality she had with her hips. One hand left her hair and trailed down the nape of her neck, her back, then landed on her ass, pulling her closer until his hardness pressed against her belly.

Hollyn moved as close as she could, reveling in the feel of his hardness against her, of the rattling feel of his chest as he growled deep, of the way his big hands felt on her. He left her ass and gripped one of her thighs, hooking it over his hip. Oooh. If only they were naked.

Noah released his grip on her hair and grabbed her other thigh, lifting her and urging her legs around his waist, never pulling his lips from hers. She gripped his hair and tugged, earning a throaty moan as he did this thing with his hips that drove her crazy as he massaged her sex through her jeans.

Setting her on the bar top, Noah pulled away and pulled her shirt over her head, nipping at her shoulder bone, the swell of her breasts until he teased her nipple through her bra with his teeth. The slight pinch sent shivers of pleasure rushing through her body.

And then he straightened so fast Hollyn almost fell off the bar.

"What are you doing?" Hollyn asked, reaching for him. So close. Just a few more items of clothing and they'd be naked.

"I won't fuck you on the bar, Hollyn," he said, pushing a rough hand through his hair.

"Why not?" she said, giving him her best sexy smile and looking up at him through her lashes.

"I don't want it to be like that for our first time."

So he'd been fantasizing about her, too. That shouldn't come as a surprise since she'd seen him sporting a boner several times since yesterday morning.

Her magic was trying its damnedest to wrap itself around Noah. Not yet. Not until she knew without a doubt that was what they both wanted. Although, she'd be lying to herself if she said she didn't want Noah forever.

Two days and something like love bloomed in her heart as she watched Noah war with his need to take her then and there and his need to make their first time together as romantic as possible. She didn't need romance, though. Never had. The things she found romantic were gestures, like when he'd carried her to his bed and slept crammed up on the couch. Or the fact he'd sat back and let her control the bar in his own place.

Or the way his eyes blazed bright amber and his hands shook with need, yet he stayed a couple feet away from her.

Fine. He was worried about their first time? She'd just take the situation into her own hands.

Sliding off the bar, she lowered to her knees, looking up at him as she undid his button then zipper. His cock sprung free the second it was no longer restrained behind his jeans. He hadn't donned boxers this morning after his shower.

Noah jerked and hissed when she lapped at the flared head, kissing away the drop of moisture glistening in the dim light in the room.

"Hollyn—"

She didn't give him a chance to protest or argue, just took his length in her mouth slowly. He was too big; she couldn't take all of him. But when she looked up in time to see his eyes roll shut, she figured she was doing just fine.

****

Noah's hand gripped the bar top as he panted. Hollyn leaned against it beside him, grinning.

"That was…" There were no words. It wasn't his first blow job, not by far. But compared to what Hollyn had just done, he was a fucking virgin before her.

She shrugged and smirked. Then she pulled her hands over her head and stretched with a wide yawn. "We almost done? I'm whipped."

Noah gaped at her. She was so nonchalant, so relaxed over the fact she'd just sucked him off behind the bar. He'd wanted to take it slow, take his time learning every single spot on her body that made her moan. He'd wanted to break the ice with a little wine, maybe some music. He wasn't exactly Don Juan, but for the first time in his adult life, he wanted to make love to a woman instead of just fucking her and running out the door.

She'd shattered that proverbial ice to smithereens the second she took him into her mouth.

"You're tired?" Noah said, a shit ton of growl lacing his words. His bear had begged to be released, at least enough to mark their mate. Noah would have to find another way to indicate to other Shifters she was taken.

Hollyn left him standing there and moved toward the door, looking at him over her shoulder with the hottest come-fuck-me look in her eyes and a soft smile on those wicked lips.

Oh, hell yeah. He might've finished, but he was ready for round two. Only this time, he wanted to hear Hollyn scream his name more than once before he found his second release. And he wanted to be buried balls deep in her when that happened. Good thing he had a stash of rubbers in his nightstand.

Noah jogged toward the door, grabbing her hand and pulling her behind him as he exited and locked the door behind him. Shit. He'd left the lights on. Who fuckin cared at that moment? All that mattered was the woman giggling beside him as he continued pulling her behind him, hoisted her into the passenger seat with his hands on her hips, then ran around the hood of his truck.

Never had he felt so out of his mind with lust that he literally ran to get to a bed faster.

Foot on the gas, he pushed the speed limit as much as he dared; he was one of the few cars out and would be targeted fast as fuck by any cops patrolling the area.

Hollyn undid her seat belt, scooted over into his space, and then redid the lap belt in the center. He lifted his arm so she could move closer to his chest. She nuzzled his neck, leaving little kisses as her hand smoothed down his chest, down his stomach, then cupped his hard again dick.

He hissed through his teeth but chuckled when Hollyn looked up at him with a hungry look.

"One taste just wasn't enough," she teased and moved to lower her head to his lap.

"Nope," he said, gently pulling her back up to a sitting position. "You're coming next. Keep your hands to yourself, woman."

Hollyn giggled a sexy sound as she ducked back out from under his arm. "Fine, big boy. I'll just sit here and behave." She'd called him that a couple of times, and each time he'd loved it even more. Now that she'd not only seen his cock but had it in her mouth, his ego swelled as much as his junk.

The closer they got to Blackwater territory, the more excited he got. And nervous. Would sex bind them? Was it another step? And why did the thought send such a thrill through his system? Stupid question; he knew exactly why that sent a thrill. He'd be tied to the woman he was already falling for and would be able to find her if some fucker got their hands on her. He'd know if she was in trouble and could get to her side to fight for and with her.

Hollyn's skin grew warmer as Noah pulled the truck up the long gravel driveway that led to all the cabins. Her magic was filling her in anticipation.

"Will it hurt?" he asked. He had no idea why that came out of his mouth. His Shift was agony, although it only last seconds. He could handle pain, especially if that pain gave him Hollyn.

"I don't know," she said. Without asking, she knew what Noah was talking about. "I can try to reel it in, though, if you want. It doesn't have to happen tonight."

Noah parked his truck and turned, cupping Hollyn's face and dipping to taste her lips for a brief second before pulling away and looking into her hypnotic eyes. "I want this, Hollyn. I want you. I know..." He took a deep breath. "We're not human. We fall faster, we know our mate right away. And you are my mate. My bear claimed you from almost the very beginning. And yeah, I'm scared shitless. I don't do commitments. I'm too busy for dating. But I promise to do everything in my power to make you happy and I *will* keep you safe." He sipped at her lips once more before pulling away and waiting for her to respond.

"I think I've loved you from the moment I saw you on your porch," she admitted and ducked her eyes. "That sounds so Hallmark chick flick-ish." A soft pink flushed her cheeks.

Where he was rushed and frantic when he left the bar, now, all he wanted was to lay her down and kiss every inch of her body starting at her feet.

Noah left the truck and rounded the hood. Hollyn was already climbing down by the time he made it to her side. He wrapped his hand around hers and led her inside. Nerves he hadn't felt since he was a teenaged virgin tickled his insides. Guiding her up the steps, he opened the door and swung it open, letting Hollyn move ahead of him.

Once they were behind closed doors, he pulled all the curtains closed then took Hollyn into his arms. He kissed her silly, nipping at her throat, her shoulder, before lifting her into his arms and carrying her down the hall and to his bedroom. He took her lips the whole trip, not wanting to break contact. He needed to feel her, taste her. Even as her lips damned near burned his, he couldn't pull away.

Laying her on his bed, he slowly undressed her while keeping his own clothes on. The next however long it took was all about Hollyn. He wanted to see her writhe on the bed, wanted to hear her breath come in pants, wanted to hear her moans. He couldn't wait to see how many sounds he could pull from her.

Noah started with her shoes, untying them and slipping them off, followed by her socks. He kissed his way up her legs until he got to the button on her pants. Nuzzling the strip of skin showing on her belly, he worked the zipper down, then laid soft kisses along her thighs as he peeled the denim off. Next was her shirt. She sat up and raised her arms so he could pull the shirt over her head. He tossed the cotton into the pile he was forming on the side of the bed.

And then Hollyn laid there like an offering in nothing but pink, lacy panties and bra.

"Fuck. You're so beautiful," he said, lying beside her and trailing his fingers over her pale flesh. Seeing her like this, on his bed, half naked with her dark as midnight hair fanned beneath her reminded him of her lineage. Her features were in such stark contrast with each other but made her all that much more appealing to him.

Hollyn smiled up at him as her legs shifted, one knee lowering and the other rising as if she were trying to create friction between her legs. Oh, he'd take care of her discomfort. That was for sure.

Leaning over her, he cupped one of her tantalizing tits in his big hand and massaged it, nipping at her nipple through her bra. He pulled the cup down to release the pink bud and lapped and sucked it. Hollyn gripped his hair and held him to her breast, arching her back beneath him. As he laved at one of her tits, he slid his hand down her soft belly until it tucked under her lacy panties. Had she intentionally worn these for him or would she be wearing this kind of stuff under her clothes all the time? And how the fuck was he supposed to concentrate if he knew the sexiness she donned beneath her pants and shirt.

When his finger touched her wet heat, he about lost his mind. Hollyn's eyes fluttered closed and her lips parted. And Noah was gone. As he dipped first one finger then the other, he came so close to losing it in his jeans. That couldn't happen. The next time he went, he wanted to be cradled between Hollyn's thighs.

Noah continued to work Hollyn with his fingers and lowered himself, pulling the pink lace down her hips with his other hand. She lifted her ass so he could remove them fully, then dropped her knees apart, giving Noah a glimpse of ecstasy.

Moving in jerky movements to keep from diving at her, Noah took a long swipe of her core and hummed in approval. So sweet. So warm. Hollyn gasped sharply and raised her arms over her head.

He spent as much time as it took between her thighs, trying to focus on anything other than the sounds coming from her mouth. He'd wanted nothing more than to hear those sounds, but now, it was about to push him over the edge.

And then, Hollyn reached down, tangled her fingers in his hair and screamed out his name. He kept lapping at her clit, working her through the aftershocks until she twitched and giggled.

He wanted to give her more, but he really didn't know how much more control he had over his body at this point. He sat back on his knees and pulled the back collar of his shirt, yanking the shirt over his head and tossed onto the growing pile. He then reached down and undid his pants, stepping off the bed to push them down his thighs and step out of them.

Hollyn watched him with heavy lids, her lips still parted as she panted from her release. Crawling back onto the bed, he grabbed a condom from the nightstand. She sat up and helped him roll it over his shaft, squeezing him once before lying back and beckoning him down.

Noah positioned himself between her thighs, dipping to take her lips as he pressed the crown against her opening. As he pushed his hips forward, they moaned in unison, the sound caught between their lips.

His bear began to scratch at his skin, begging to be let out, begging to mark their mate. *Too dangerous*, he told his beast. They had no idea what a Shifter's bite would do to a Fairy and he sure as fuck wasn't going to experiment with Hollyn.

Hollyn's arms tightened around his back as her ankles hooked around his ass. She lifted her hips and met him thrust for thrust. They needed to slow down. He was too close. She was so tight and warm, almost too warm. Her magic. It was trying to tie itself to him. When Hollyn opened her eyes next, they were a striking violet, lighter than the amethyst color he'd seen before.

"You sure?" she asked, her voice throaty and full of lust and emotion.

He nodded and bent to take her lips again, his hips keeping the same motion. His body grew warm, warmer until he felt feverish. It bordered on uncomfortable. But all he really cared about was Hollyn wrapped around him, clenching him as another release rippled through her. She threw her head back, opened her mouth, and this time, when she screamed, a wave of power flowed over him, moving his hair, rippling the curtains as if a hard wind had blown through the room.

His balls tightened as his release crashed into him, rolling over him, stealing his breath as Hollyn's magic squeezed his heart. For a brief second, he felt like he was dying. But what a way to go.

And then the wind died down, Hollyn relaxed back against the pillow, her eyes rolling shut, and Noah was able to breathe again. The need to mark Hollyn was still strong, but now, there were so many other emotions floating through him he couldn't think straight. Fear. Anger. Lust. Love. Affection. He was feeling Hollyn deep inside, feeling her emotions in real time.

He hated that she still felt fear, even though she didn't show it, even though she was good at hiding that shit. But the fact he could feel how she felt about him, the fact he could feel how embedded in her heart he'd become, that erased everything else. Even if she was afraid of being found, Noah knew she was safe with him.

"I can feel you," Noah said with wonder.

"Well, you are still buried inside of me," she teased, peeking at him through one open lid.

Noah chuckled. This woman made him laugh more in the last two days than he had in months. He kissed the tip of her nose and pulled from her, earning a disappointed groan.

Turning his back, he removed the condom and disposed of it in the trash can next to his bed.

"I just realized how clean your bedroom is," Hollyn said.

Noah glanced back at her. She was pushed up onto her elbows and looking around his room. "Because I don't spend much time in here. I tend to strip as I'm making my way to the shower after work and then just kind of fall into bed. You're lucky I happened to pull on a pair of boxers before bed that night," he teased.

Hollyn smiled up at him. "I wouldn't have minded getting an eyeful."

Noah shook his head as he smiled down at the woman who was now permanently tied to him. "My animal wants to mark you. But I'm scared of what will happen," he admitted after a few moments of studying her face. It was like he was seeing her for the first time all over again. Not only could he feel her, feel every single emotion that floated through her heart, including the rush of anxiety at him admitting his animal wanted to mark her, but he could see her differently. She was more beautiful and he could see the tiny features that separated her from humans, something he hadn't noticed before now. Her nose was a little longer, her ears a little pointier, and the color of her eyes were even more obvious now.

"I don't know, either. It could kill me. Or it could do nothing."

Nope. Not worth the risk.

"How bad is it?" Hollyn asked, rolling onto her side and propping her cheek on her palm.

For some reason, there was no awkwardness, even though it was their first time together. It felt normal, natural, as if they'd made love thousands of times. It was because their souls already knew each other before their bodies ever touched. He knew that. And he didn't give a fuck how sappy that sounded.

"How bad is what?" he asked, lying beside her and turning to look into her face.

She lowered onto the pillow so they were eye to eye.

"You said your bear wants to mark me. Is it because of my magic? Did I freak him out?"

Noah snorted out a sound. "He's wanted to mark you since yesterday morning. He declared you mate right away."

"You should've said something," Hollyn said, her lids growing heavy. She yawned wide, giggling when Noah raised a brow at her.

"What should I have said? We just met, and this is crazy—"

"Here's my number. Call me maybe."

Noah frowned down at her. Was she falling asleep and talking through a dream?

"What?"

"It's a song. You never heard it?"

Raising his hand, he pushed her hair behind her ear and let his eyes roam her face. She was getting slap happy. She used to be a bar tender, but it had been a few weeks. And she'd worked her ass off today. And he could only imagine how tiring that kind of use of magic was to her body.

"Sleep. We'll talk tomorrow," Noah grumbled, lifting enough to press a kiss to her temple before pulling her to his chest. He tucked her under his chin and wrapped both arms around her, sighing with contentment when he felt her heart warm for him. He swore her heartbeat to the exact same rhythm his did now.

Noah listened to Hollyn's slow, steady breathing and let the sound lull him to sleep. This was the first night in he didn't know how many years he'd go to bed excited to wake up the next day. And it had everything to do with his mate sleeping in his arms.

Chapter Seven

Hollyn had had a case of perma-smile for the past two weeks. Her life had become like a fairy tale, no pun intended. Of course, it wasn't the kind of fairy tale humans dreamed of. She was bound to a Shifter who doted on her and even started trying to pick up after himself and put his dirty dishes in the dishwasher.

And he seemed lighter, happier, and he smiled more now. It probably had something to do with the fact he was able to sit with his friends when she was working the bar. He was able to relax more and trusted her to run her side of his business while Shawnee waited tables. Occasionally, he'd have to head into the kitchen to cook lunch, but most people these days were coming in for the show. They just couldn't believe Noah had hired a human and had heard the stories of how she performed while she tended the bar and had to come see it for themselves. She was cleaning up in tips.

She'd bought herself a few more outfits and shoes. And of course, a few more sexy, lacy bras and panties. She loved the look in Noah's eyes when she stripped for bed and he got a look at them. They'd made love at least once a day since that first time. She couldn't get enough of him. And since she could feel his emotions, she knew he felt the same way. It was the closest a couple could get to telepathy. They didn't even have to ask the other if they were in the mood; she could feel Noah's arousal the second he looked at her.

And she could feel how strongly he felt about her. He loved her. And even though she'd felt that love from the moment she closed the bond, it had grown every day. She loved him, too. She never thought she could feel so strongly about someone so quickly. Oh, who was she kidding. She never thought she'd fall so in love with a man ever.

That was how her life had become a fairy tale. It was like they lived in their own world, made their own rules, and counted down the minutes every day until they could be in each other's arms again.

"Hey bar wench," Nova called out. Everyone at the table, including Noah, turned and frowned at her. "What? I can't think of another name for her." That was because Noah and Hollyn had only told his own Clan about Hollyn's Fae lineage. He obviously trusted his friends, but the fewer people who knew, the less risk there was of someone slipping at the wrong time.

"Whatcha need, Nova?" Hollyn called from the bar, her eyes on the drink she was pouring. Hardly anyone ordered beers anymore. They all wanted to see Hollyn's tricks.

"Cookout tomorrow?" Nova called back.

Hollyn had worked every single day that Noah had. In other words, she'd worked seven days a week for the last two weeks. Fourteen consecutive days.

"I think I'm working tomorrow," Hollyn called back, sliding the glass across the bar and accepting cash from her customer. There were a few who came in almost every night, but periodically, new faces would wander in. Those were the ones who made her nervous. Even Noah said he didn't know them, but he'd said there were a lot of Shifters living in Jefferson County. Something she would've never guessed during her trip there. She'd had them all pegged as humans.

"Noah could always shut down for the day. Tomorrow's Sunday. It's supposed to be a day of rest," Nova said to a chorus of boos and hisses. The customers didn't like the thought of Moe's being closed, even for a day.

"Hey!" Noah boomed over the noise. "If my mate needs a day off, then she's getting a fucking day off," Noah yelled, his bear evident in the growly sound of his words. His bear had become a little unstable over past few weeks, its need to mark Hollyn almost crippling. They'd tried different things, letting Noah nibble on her neck with his teeth, not showering after sex in hopes if she was covered in his scent his bear might calm down. Nothing worked.

The room went quiet at his announcement. They hadn't told anyone, and since he couldn't mark her, she didn't carry the change in her blood that she would if he'd left a scar on her shoulder. But anyone who spent more than five minutes with them could tell they were crazy about each other.

"Holy shit!" Reed said with a burst of laughter. "That's freaking awesome!" He clapped Noah on the shoulder. "I didn't scent you on her," he said, and Hollyn jerked her eyes to Noah's to see how he'd cover that one.

"We're doing things our own way, fucker. We don't have to follow stupid rules." Noah met her gaze and winked and her heart warmed. She felt Noah's joy through their bond. She felt everything. Including the jolt of fear when Reed had mentioned her lack of his mark. He never looked around to see if anyone was paying attention, never outwardly looked as if he had a care in the world, but she'd felt it.

It had taken him almost a solid week to get used to feeling her inside of him. She'd feared he'd go insane; it had happened in the past. Sometimes, the emotions were so strong the person carrying both could lose his marbles.

But Noah was strong, stronger than any human she'd ever met, stronger than the few Fae she'd known in her life. Now, he relished the feeling of her heart beating in time with his, relished feeling how she felt about him, relished never having to wonder if their love was real.

"I wouldn't mind a day off, too," Shawnee said from beside the bar. Noah had warned her that Shawnee was a bit of a workaholic but it was mainly because she hadn't been allowed to do anything for herself her whole life. It was like she was making up for lost time.

Hollyn raised her brows at Noah and smiled. She was tired. And her feet hurt. And most importantly, she hadn't been able to spend more than a few hours with Noah other than at work since day one. It would be nice to just unwind and hang out with some friends and maybe spend some time with him on the couch.

"Fuck it. We're closed tomorrow, assholes," Noah yelled.

She winced again. She hated when he talked to the customers like that, but they didn't seem to mind. Where he was gruff and a tad surly with everyone else, he was downright sweet and tender with Hollyn. Hell, he softened around all the women, but they never saw the gentle side of him.

Another round of boos filled the room, but they kept laughing, drinking and having a good time.

It seemed like in a blink of an eye it was time to close. Big River and all of Blackwater had begun to stay after close recently, as if wanting to aid in protecting Hollyn. It made her feel good. It made her feel like she was really part of the family. And since Noah and she had closed the bond, she kind of was, even if Noah's bear couldn't get his way.

They all helped Shawnee clean the tables, stack the chairs, and sweep and mop the floor. Noah and Hollyn worked shoulder to shoulder, restocking the beer cooler, cleaning and putting away glasses, and then cleaning the kitchen. It was probably as domestic as they would ever get since they both worked so much.

When the place was clean, they all filed outside. Hollyn stretched her back as she walked. There was an odd feeling to the air, like static before a storm. She looked around, searching for clouds or lightening in the distance, but the sky was clear.

"What's wrong?" Emory asked, looking up at the sky with Hollyn.

"Nothing. Thought a storm was coming," Hollyn said, nudging Emory with her shoulder. "Thanks for the help tonight. You guys are all so sweet for helping us get the place cleaned up faster."

"Thank Shawnee," Nova said with a wink.

Frowning at Nova, Hollyn asked, "Why would I thank Shawnee?" After all, Shawnee was a paid employee. She was supposed to help clean up if she closed with Hollyn and Noah.

"Because she thinks if you two get more time at home, there will be cubs sooner," Reed blurted out just before he said, "Ouch!" when Gray cuffed him upside the back of the head. "What? That's what she said. I'm just the messenger."

Lola giggled and wrapped an arm around his waist, smiling back at Hollyn as they climbed into one of the trucks the wolves had driven.

"Shawnee!" Hollyn said then turned to Noah. "Did you hear that? Shawnee is trying to get me knocked up!" Noah's lips twitched as he tried to hold in a laugh. She jabbed a finger in his direction. "You realize that means she's listening to see if we boink every night."

"Ew!" Callie said as she and Micah passed.

That didn't help Noah's held back smile. He just chuckled and shook his head. "Then she's going to get an earful tonight," Noah said as he lunged at Hollyn pretending to miss as she ducked out of the way.

She knew he could catch her if he wanted, but she liked when they were able to play. She liked her new life. She liked that she was able to enjoy her new family, she was able to enjoy her new mate, her new Clan without fear.

Half lie. Now, instead of fearing for her own safety, she feared someone would come in and take all of them away from her. And that, she couldn't survive.

****

Hollyn rolled onto her side. She was alone. Reaching for his side of the bed, she smiled sleepily at the warmth still on the sheets. He hadn't been up long. Hollyn rolled until her face was buried in his pillow and inhaled his scent. She loved the way he smelled.

Reaching deep, she used her magic to locate the love of her life. Her smile grew wider as those words bounced around her head. Love of her life. She'd been lucky enough to find him.

Noah was in the kitchen, but he wasn't happy. She could almost feel his growl all the way in the bedroom, even if she couldn't hear it.

Throwing the blankets off, she dressed quickly – they'd showered when they got home and then again after they'd made love – and sought out her man.

He was sitting at the kitchen table, his head in his hands. Every muscle in his body was strung tight and she could see him tremble lightly. What had set him off? They'd had a wonderful night and were supposed to head into Big River later that afternoon.

"Hey," she said softly but he still jumped a little. Lowering in the chair beside him, she reached out and laid her hand on his bare back. "What's wrong? What happened?"

A growl worked up his chest and trickled through his lips. "Bear," he said. Just the one word.

She'd known his bear was trying to force a Shift to mark Hollyn. All it would take was a partial Shift of his teeth. But Noah was growing concerned his bear would take his skin and mark her in its animal form. That could seriously injure her, whether or not it poisoned her.

"I can try to find someone who would know, Noah. I can see if any of my parents' friends are still alive, see what would happen –"

"No," he said, his voice gravelly. "Don't want anyone to know you're here."

His teeth were clenched so tightly she feared he'd break a tooth.

"There's got to be another way he can mark me without his teeth," Hollyn said, rubbing small circles on Noah's back. He never relaxed under her touch. In fact, the trembling seemed to increase.

"I love you. But I think you need to leave," he said, turning glowing amber eyes on her. They faded to brown, back to amber, back to brown. He was fighting his animal.

"Bear," she called to his animal, standing and putting a couple of feet between them.

"What are you doing?" Noah said, gripping the table as if trying to hold himself down.

"Bear and I need to have a talk. He needs to understand. He needs to know I'm not going anywhere. I'm bound to both of you, Noah. I'm Bear's, too."

His eyes flashed bright amber and then he was on his feet. Shit. She hadn't thought about the fact Noah could be pushed to the background when the bear took over. He was still in there, but right now, it was his bear watching her, stalking her as she backed away.

Holding her hands out, she raised her chin and stopped moving. If she ran, he'd just chase her. And Noah would never forgive himself if he wasn't able to control his bear and Hollyn got hurt.

"Listen to me, Bear." He took another step closer to her, his nostrils flaring as he scented the air around her. "What do you need? Tell me. Because you're hurting Noah. And if you hurt Noah, you're hurting me."

"Mark you. Mine," he growled out. His teeth began to Shift.

Shit. Shit shit shit.

"No, Bear. If you bite me, you'll kill me. Do you understand that? If you bite me, you'll lose your mate. And you'll hurt Noah."

Noah, or Bear – he still looked like Noah, but she couldn't seem to find him in the person watching her now – stopped moving, his brows creased. A deep, scary growl worked up his throat, deeper and louder than she'd heard Noah make yet.

"There has to be another way, Bear. Another way for you to mark me without your teeth."

Noah's eyes bled back to brown. Bear had retreated for a moment. It was just Hollyn and Noah.

"Is he gone? Did I get through to him?"

"Hollyn," he said, a look of regret flashed through him the same time it hit her square in the heart. Before anything happened, she knew what was going through Noah's mind. And she realized it was the same thing going through his bear's. He'd found a way to mark her without tearing her skin.

Noah's lips crashed down on Hollyn's. His arm snaked around her back and he bent her backward as he deepened the kiss. When he pulled away, it wasn't Noah's warm brown eyes looking at her, but his bear's amber glow.

She knew it wasn't fully Noah touching her now, but she didn't care. She'd meant what she'd said. She was bound to them both, loved them both. Her heart, mind, soul, and her body belonged to them both.

Noah's hands were hurried and frantic as he stripped her shorts and tank top off, yanking at the seam at her hip and ripping her panties away. The fabric fluttered to the ground as Noah lifted Hollyn, his hands tight on her thighs, and wrapped her legs around his waist.

In one thrust, Noah entered her, pulling a cry of pleasure from her mouth. He walked them across the room until her back hit the wall and continued to pump into her. Holy shit. She was already so close. Part of her thought maybe she should be weirded out by the glowing eyes staring at her as he took her against the wall. But the bigger part, the part so in love with this man, accepted this side of him, just like everything else about him.

Pulling her from the wall, he walked her across the room, his cock still buried deep, and laid her on the couch. He lifted onto his knees, and spread her thighs further apart, watching where they were connected. His eyes bled to brown long enough that Hollyn knew he could feel and see everything. He smiled down at her, then his eyes flashed bright again.

Throwing her head back, Hollyn cried out with her release. Just as she was descending from her high, Noah pulled from her, took himself in his hand, and covered her in his release. He was marking her in the only way he could think that wouldn't endanger her. He was covering her in his scent, in the rawest way possible.

Noah stared down at Hollyn as his eyes bled back to brown. "You okay?" he asked, his voice still gravelly, but she could feel his pain residing as more joy bloomed.

"I'm better than okay," she said, holding her arms out to him.

He looked at the mess on her stomach, then back to her eyes. So fast she squealed in surprise, Noah scooped her from the couch and carried her to the shower. He kept his back to the spray as the water warmed, then turned her and cleaned his release from her stomach. Another tender, sweet moment.

"Is that going to freak Bear out?" she asked, lowering her eyes to watch his hands roam her body and wonder if they'd ever get tired of touching each other.

"Nah," he said, turning her away from the spray as he ended the spray. He toweled her off, lowering to his knees and burying his face in her stomach. "I can still smell it. It's not quite the blood change, but you'll carry my scent for a while."

Okay. So all they had to do when his bear started to get antsy was let Noah release on her body. And that thought turned her on. That had been one of the hottest things ever. It was the primality of it, the desperation in his eyes. She felt herself getting turned again and realized it was Noah. Or maybe it was both of them. As his eyes roamed her naked body, she figured it didn't matter.

****

Noah kept glancing at Hollyn as she rode shot gun, her window down, her hair blowing around her face like a crazy woman. They'd found a loop hole. His bear had found a way to mark their mate without endangering her. It might not be as permanent as leaving the scar on her shoulder, but it would do.

Shawnee and Colton rode in the backseat. Shawnee kept shooting Noah looks in the mirror. He knew what she wanted to know. Was Hollyn pregnant? Hell no, she wasn't. He knew what would happen if she ever got pregnant; their children would be hunted even more than the Fae. And he would never put a child in danger, not if he could avoid it.

"So," Noah said, keeping his eyes on the road. "You and Colton thinking about kids?"

Hollyn barked out a laugh and turned to look at Shawnee. "Yeah. You pregnant yet? I mean, you're the one who wants cubs in the Clan so bad."

Shawnee's face went red enough that her freckles paled.

"I keep saying I'm ready to try," Colton said, wrapping an arm around her shoulders.

"I just want more time with Colton first. That's all," Shawnee said, slinking down in her seat as if trying to hide from all the attention.

"Yeah, well. I've only had two weeks with Noah. Maybe when we've been together as long as you two, we'll think about kids." She turned and winked at Noah.

Wow. She was actually thinking about growing a family? They hadn't discussed it, but he'd just figured she'd ruled that out from day one.

"Whatever. I'm ready for some little Fairy babies to fill the territory. Just imagine how—"

"Please don't talk about that when we get to Big River," Hollyn said, turning and pleading Shawnee.

"No one else knows, Shawnee," Noah said, his voice apparently too hard for Colton. He growled a warning and glared at Noah in the rearview mirror.

"I know that," Shawnee said. "Did you really think I was going to blab it to everyone?"

"Just… don't let it slip. Or whatever," Hollyn said. "Pleeease?" she added to soften the words.

Shawnee smiled and rolled her eyes.

Carter and Luke pulled their truck into Big River ahead of Noah. Everyone was there, including a few lionesses from the Pride on the top of the hill. He didn't know them well, but he knew enough to be happy they were getting out of the territory and hanging out with everyone.

"About time," Nova called out as they all piled out of their trucks.

Noah and Colton grabbed some lawn chairs and their blue cooler from the back of his truck and followed Shawnee and Hollyn to the circle of people. Noah took the opportunity to check out her ass.

Once all the chairs were added to the circle and the cooler was set close enough to grab what they needed, Noah sat beside Hollyn who'd sat beside Reed.

Reed turned wide eyes on Hollyn. "He finally marked you?" he asked, his grin growing wide. "After all that talk about *we make our own rules*?" Reed said, imitating Noah's gruff voice.

"Shut up," Noah said, handing a beer to Hollyn.

"Where is it?" Lola asked, leaning forward to see past her mate, Reed.

"What?" Hollyn asked. She'd heard her. Noah could feel the spike in anxiety as she tried to think of a lie.

"Where's your mark. I thought bears usually marked their mates so everyone could see."

Hollyn's mouth opened but nothing came out. So Noah stepped in. "I marked her where only I can see. Like I said, making our own rules."

"That's hot," Nova said, pointing at them with her beer bottle.

"You realize that means you're going to end up in a book, right?" Emory said with a smile and a shake of her head.

"Um, being as I've been forbidden to write about Shifters, don't you think it'd be a little weird if I had some human country boy biting his girlfriend?" Nova said with a *duh* expression all over her face.

Hollyn laughed and his heart swelled even more. When she felt it, she looked at Noah with the mushiest look in her eyes, as if trying to tell him *I love you* without saying a word. *Love you more,* he tried to send back, even though she wouldn't hear the words.

Everyone fell into their usual banter and jokes. Nova and Lola swapped war stories of being kept up by their daughters. Reed asked Hollyn about her bartending experience. Callie teased Micah about something he'd done the night before. The women all teased Carter and Luke about pairing up. In the meantime, the beer, Jager, and vodka flowed easily. Noah and Carter would have to stay sober to drive everyone home. That, or they'd either have to crash at one of the wolves' homes – which none of them were big enough for the bears' big bodies – or Shift and run back to their territory through the woods. It wasn't always possible to call on their animals when they were inebriated. And by the look of everyone around him, they were flying past the inebriated stage and straight into trashed.

Hollyn was cracking him up, laughing freely and joining in the ribbing. She fit in perfectly with his friends. She'd told him a few days ago that these people were the closest to a family she'd had since she was young. He'd felt her affection for them as she spoke, but he'd also felt her sadness at her loss. It was something she'd yet to tell him about. And he wouldn't push her. When she was ready, she'd open up to him and tell him what happened to her people.

"Oh, I've dropped more than a few bottles," Hollyn was telling Peyton. "When I first started doing this, I used to take home empty bottles and practice in the alley beside my apartment building. I used to get so much crap from the landlord. Even though I was cleaning up the broken glass."

"Did you ever get cut?" Callie asked. She was snuggled into Micah's side as the sun began to set. It was getting late in the season and the evenings were growing cooler.

"Oh my gosh. So many times. I swear I wore Band-aids for weeks when I started at my first bar."

"How many places have you worked?" Peyton asked.

Hollyn chewed on the inside of her cheek as she mentally counted. "Ten, I think."

"Wow. Job hopper," Reed teased.

Hollyn tensed. "I was always on the run. I changed jobs every time I changed cities."

Okay. She was revealing a lot. He needed to gently guide her to a different topic.

"Someone light the fire, please. I'm freezing," Callie said, wrapping her arms around her middle.

Reed moved to grab the lighter from the grill, but Hollyn, drunk and not thinking, leaned forward. “I got it,” she said, and before Noah could stop her, reached her hand forward and called forward a flame, blowing it toward the waiting wood.

All conversation ceased. The bears looked at her with worry on their faces. Everyone else looked shocked. Shit.

“Hollyn” he said, grabbing her hand and pushing it to her lap. The flame burned him as he closed his hand around hers, but she didn’t seem phased. Of course not; the fire was a part of who she was. That was why her skin grew so hot when they made love. It coursed through her veins, just like her blood.

“What?” she asked, turning unfocused eyes on Noah.

“Holy shit,” Nova breathed out.

“Did that just happen?” Emory said.

“What are you?” Micah asked, too much growl in his voice for Noah’s liking.

Noah snarled at Micah, but kept his hand wrapped around Hollyn’s. Within a few seconds, the burn faded as her fire died out.

“Uh oh,” Hollyn said, turning her eyes up to his face. “I didn’t mean to do that.”

Noah smiled at her, but it was forced. He didn’t want her to think he was mad at her. It wasn’t that he didn’t want his friends to know. He just didn’t want them to have to carry her —

“I’m a Fairy!”

Secret.

Noah’s eyes closed and he shook his head. Maybe he’d get lucky and everyone was drunk enough they’d forget by morning.

“What the fuck,” Micah said.

Noah opened his eyes and turned them on Micah. “Problem?”

“Is she being hunted? Is that why she’s here?”

“I told you Aron brought her to me for protection,” Noah said, his muscles tensing.

“You didn’t tell us she was being fucking hunted. What happens if they come here? What happens if the women are home alone with the pups?”

"Well, for one thing, we have Cujo," Nova piped in, oblivious to the riled up males staring each other down.

"And I have this," Hollyn said, opening her free hand and producing a flame that licked high into the sky. "They won't sneak up on me this time."

"Hollyn," Noah warned. Fuck. This was getting out of hand.

"What? Might as well tell them everything now. Some assholes snuck up on me and stabbed me with a needle. They drugged me because they knew I'd kick their asses." Her smile was wobbly, her speech was slurred, but Noah could feel the anger from her kidnapping through their connection.

"Did you mark her?" Micah asked, never turning his glare away. "Did you really mark her?"

"You can smell it from there," Noah said, his jaw clenching as his bear growled in his head. *Protect my mate.*

Our *mate*, Noah reminded him.

"Is she going to be danger to the Pack?" Micah asked.

"Micah, calm the fuck down," Gray said, rising slowly to stand between the two men.

Noah watched as each guy whispered something in their mates' ears. They each stood, rounded the chairs, and urged Hollyn back and away from the circle. His bear didn't like them taking her away from him. But his human side knew they were trying to protect her.

"She's in my territory," Carter said. "She's under our protection."

"She's here, isn't she?"

"Micah," Callie said, staying closer to Micah than the rest of the women. "You thought I was going to be a threat, too."

"And me," Nova said.

"Pretty sure he thought that about me, too," Peyton said.

"Well, you are kind of scary," Emory said from behind Noah.

Tristan glanced in his mate's direction and shook his head. He didn't say much. They'd all learned last year that he stuttered and feared being judged. Even though they all accepted him just as he was, the dude still rarely spoke more than a word at a time.

"Calm down," he said, presumably to Peyton.

If Peyton felt Hollyn was at risk, her wolf would charge out of her and go after whoever the perceived threat was, and ,currently, that threat was Micah.

"We'll leave," Carter said, putting a hand on Noah's chest to keep him from moving forward.

"Why do you have to be such an asshole all the time?" Nova said. "You always pick fights with everyone. Can't we just have a good time for once? I don't see any asshole standing in the woods ready to start shit, do you?" Nova said, putting her hands to her eyes and pretending to scour the woods. Noah was pretty sure even if someone was standing in the middle of the field, she'd be too drunk to see him clearly.

Micah's eyes finally flicked over to Nova, then moved over the group of women waiting to see if there'd be a full out brawl. Shame flashed through his eyes as he sought out his own mate.

"Fuck," he muttered under his breath. The glow in his eyes faded and he lowered to his chair.

"We good?" Noah grumbled, his bear still aching to get out.

Micah nodded once; a muscle ticked in his jaw. He was fighting his already volatile animal. If he Shifted, there was no way Noah could keep his bear in his skin.

"Why can't we ever just have one normal get together," Nova grumbled as she retook her seat next to Gray. Her butt was only halfway in the seat when a small cry came from inside. "Great. You woke up Rieka. Good job, guys," Nova said, glaring at Noah then Micah.

"Sorry."

"Sorry," Micah and Noah grumbled at the same time.

Noah hadn't noticed the baby monitor sitting at Reed's feet. For a brief second, Noah had been so freaked out by Hollyn outing herself and the possible fight with one his own damn friends, he'd forgotten all about the pups living there. Rieka was a few months shy of three and little Grace would be one next month.

Maybe Micah was right. Maybe it was too dangerous to have Hollyn around Big River. Carter, Luke, and Colton already pledged their fealty and protection, as did Shawnee. But that didn't mean he needed to bring her to the wolves' territory. What if? What if someone did find her? What if they were able to track her here? The women would fight, there was no doubt about that, but they'd have to protect the babies. He couldn't live with himself if anything happened to any of them, especially the little girls.

And now, every single person sitting there knew what she was, knew what kind of magic she held.

"So you didn't really mark her, then," Micah said.

"Dude! We really doing this again?" Reed said, his usual laid back and playful manner fading and replaced by anger.

"Not an accusation. Just a question."

Peyton still stood close to Hollyn. She had never sat after everything calmed down. Which meant Tristan stood with her.

"Scent," Tristan said. "Covered her."

Noah glanced over the back of the chair and nodded at Tristan. "Yeah."

"Can't mark her," Tristan said, looking up at Micah. "Poison."

Peyton's eyes instantly flashed to their glowing aqua color, red rimming her pupils.

"No one poisoned her. She's safe," Callie said, trying to slow Peyton down before she exploded into her psychotic wolf. She even tried to stand, but Micah shook his head and pulled her back down. Callie was one of the few people in the Pack who Peyton's wolf wouldn't attack. The theory was that her wolf saw Callie as weak, as needing protection.

"No one poisoned me, Peyton," Hollyn slurred, turning in her chair to look at Peyton who stood sentry over. "You can relax. I don't think I can handle Cujo tonight." She smiled up at Peyton, but it looked forced. In fact, Hollyn wasn't looking all that great. She looked a little pale, as if maybe she'd had a little too much to drink.

"You okay?" he asked her, leaning into her space a little to whisper in her ear.

"Yep. Dandy."

"Uh oh. Looks like we got ourselves another lightweight," Reed teased.

Hollyn scowled in his direction. "I'm not a lightweight. I just forgot to eat today."

Shit. He hadn't even noticed she hadn't eaten. He'd been too busy worshipping her body. He hadn't eaten, either, but that was normal for him. No food in her belly and a shit ton of booze; no wonder she was so drunk.

"Nova got drunk at Moe's once and Shifted. She went after someone she thought was an asshole," Reed explained to Hollyn.

"He was an asshole," Gray said, looking up at his house. His mate still hadn't come back outside. Now that Noah had Hollyn, he understood the need to always have her nearby, always needing to touch her, always needing to see her face.

As Hollyn nodded as Reed told her the story, his own stomach began to churn with nausea. And he knew it wasn't from alcohol. He'd barely had anything to drink. And since Shifters didn't get sick, that meant…

"Excuse me," she said in the middle of Reed's story and lunged to her feet.

She swayed and Noah jumped up to keep her from falling face first into the fire and escorted her away from everyone else. When she was far enough away, she doubled over and grabbed her hair in one fist. Noah stood by, rubbing small circles on her back. Nothing came up at first. She just stood there, panting heavily.

A sharp pain hit his stomach, the roiling kicked up, then Hollyn double over again, vomiting in the drying grass.

"Ohhh!" everyone said, turning quickly to keep from seeing the disgusting show.

He didn't quite feel the puke coming up, but he felt every single second of misery Hollyn felt. She tilted her head to look up at him and caught him with his arm around his stomach.

"Warned you," she said, then turned quickly when another wave hit her.

As much as he loved every second of being magic bound to Hollyn, this was something he hoped he never had to go through again. And then another thought hit him: If they ever decided to have children, would he feel the labor pains, too? Maybe there was more than one huge reason to refrain from parenthood.

Chapter Eight

Hollyn woke to Noah sitting on the side of the bed, his hand pressed against her forehead. Peeling her lids back, she groaned when the bright light made her head throb.

"Yeah. Sucks," Noah grumbled in his gruff voice.

Opening her eyes again, guilt hit her hard when she got a good look at Noah. He looked like hell. And he hadn't drank. He was getting a front row seat to Hollyn's hangover.

"I'm never drinking again," she muttered as she rolled over and pulled the pillow over her head.

"If you're working today, it's time to get up. Unless you want to work in your birthday suit."

Hollyn lifted her head and looked down at her naked body. "Did we..."

"No. You were too drunk. You just stripped naked, smiled wide, then collapsed onto the bed." His lips twitched as he held back his amusement.

Hollyn groaned again, this time out of embarrassment. Had she attempted to seduce Noah and passed out instead? Or had she just gotten naked for bed? She never slept naked. She always made sure she was covered enough in case she had to run.

"Sorry," she mumbled and sat up. Shit. The room spun no matter how hard Hollyn tried to focus on the dresser across the room.

"Do you remember anything from last night?" Noah asked, handing her a glass of water. "All of it," he said when she took a sip.

Hollyn down the glass of cool water. It helped a little, but she needed a whole bottle of Pepto Bismol and a few handfuls of Tylenol. "A little."

Noah studied her for a minute, his eyes narrowed.

"Do you remember starting the fire with your magic then telling the entire group you're a Fairy?"

As he spoke, she felt his fear grow with each syllable. If those people were his friends, if he trusted them as much as he said, why was he afraid of them knowing.

"Do you think one of them would say something?" she asked, clutching the empty cool glass between her hands.

He must've feared she'd break the glass and gently extricated it from her hands, setting it on the nightstand beside the bed.

"Not on purpose." He was using the same gruff tone he used with customers at Moe's. He was not happy with her. But it was more than being mad; his fear was making her heart speed up.

"I need you to calm down, Noah. I feel too yucky to deal with your emotions, too," she admitted. She lowered her head into her hands. She had to get out of bed. She needed a shower before work. And if Noah was going in, she could, too. She knew he felt as bad as she did and he'd hardly had anything to drink. It wasn't fair to him.

Noah watched her as she threw the blankets off and stood, grabbing anything nearby to keep steady. He reached for her, but dropped his hand when she swatted it away.

As she shuffled to the bathroom, one hand on the wall, she realized how shitty she was being to him. She'd apologize after. For now, she was focusing on not puking again. The last thing she wanted to do was make Noah feel worse.

But she had warned him. She'd warned him he'd feel her emotions, he'd feel anytime she was in pain. She just hadn't thought about the fact Shifters didn't get sick. He'd finally know how it felt if she ever got a virus. He'd feel every ache and pain. Poor guy.

As she showered, she tried to conjure memories of last night. She'd actually used her magic in front of everyone, then proceeded to tell them exactly what she was. Great. And he feared one of them might slip in front of the wrong people.

But what worried her was the fact there were more people to keep her secret. Why the hell had Aron brought her here? He knew how close knit these people were, he knew there were cubs in the wolf Pack. Why would he risk his friends' lives?

Fate. That word bounced around inside her head again. She'd wondered before if her magic hadn't let her get caught because it knew what was coming. Her magic knew Noah was waiting for her, even if he didn't know he was looking for her.

If it was fate that brought Noah and Hollyn together, that had to mean all the people her magic had brought into her life would be safe. Right?

Something like anger bubbled up deep inside of her. She followed the thread; not her anger. Noah was angry at something or someone. Was his bear getting restless again? As hot as his way of marking her was, she wasn't in the mood. She worried if she even tried to make love to Noah, she'd end up puking on him. Not exactly sexy.

Hollyn ended the spray and scrubbed off with the towel. Once her hair and teeth were brushed, she forewent the makeup for the day, and headed to the bedroom to get dressed. She wanted to be completely covered when she sought out Noah. Just in case.

Dressed with shoes on, she pushed off the bed. The glass of water and shower made her feel closer to normal, but it would be at least a day before she got rid of all the symptoms of her hangover.

Nope. Never drinking again.

Noah was standing in the gravel in front of the cabin, his arms crossed over his chest. Carter stood across from him, Luke leaned against the truck, and Colton leaned against the railing. All four of them looked pissed.

As she stepped onto the porch, all four sets of eyes jerked to her. "Where's Shawnee?" Hollyn asked instead of diving straight into the whole *what the hell was going on*?

"Getting ready for work," Colton said, a smile tipping the corners of his lips. The anger was still evident in the faint glow in his eyes, but he was one of those people who always looked happy.

When no one said anything else, just kept staring at her like they were waiting for her to go back inside, she slapped her hands on her hips. "This is obviously about me. I could feel your anger in the shower."

Noah looked away; his jaw clenched so tight she worried he'd crack a molar.

"What's going on?" she asked.

"Other than Big River, have you told anyone else about…your heritage?" Carter asked, wording it carefully. There was no reason; the four Shifters standing around knew before she'd ever blabbed.

"No. Why?"

"You're sure," Carter said. "You never used your magic at the bar?"

Hollyn turned her attention to Noah as that anger he'd felt inside mixed with fear. A lot of it. "Other than fire breathing, no. And they all think I'm blowing alcohol. It's a fairly popular trick. No way would anyone put two and two together from just that."

"Well, someone did," Carter said, rubbing the back of his neck.

Luke's eyes blazed brighter than Hollyn had ever seen them and he looked like he was strung tight as a bow. She no longer feared any of the Shifters she'd come to know, but at that moment, Luke was pretty freaking scary.

"What?" she asked when her throat threatened to close. "Just tell me."

"Aron called," Carter said. "The assholes he was chasing disappeared. He got word they were spotted heading this way."

"They're coming here?" Hollyn whispered. She couldn't make her voice any louder. She could barely breathe. She looked at Noah, looked at the people who had taken her in and given her a family. She needed to go. She needed to run far away from them. She needed to lure the danger away from the people she loved more than herself.

Noah's hand went to his chest and he winced. He could feel her pain at the thought of leaving them behind. He could feel her trying to break the bond. If he couldn't feel her, he couldn't follow her, and he'd be safe.

"What are you doing?" Noah gritted out between clenched teeth.

Shit. She was causing him too much pain. But it needed to be done. It was the only way to protect him.

"Hollyn," he said, climbing the steps and pulling her into his arms, wrapping himself around her as much as he could. "You're safe. Nothing's going to happen. Stop."

What did he think he felt? What did he think she was doing? Did he think it was a mere case of fear causing that ache? It didn't matter.

With him holding her like that she realized there was no way she could successfully sever the magic between them. It was too strong. Their connection was too strong.

And she loved him too much.

Did he realize she wasn't afraid for herself? Not anymore. She had her magic. She had her fire. She feared for the Shifters, for the bear Clan, for the wolf Pack, for the babies. She feared for her family. She feared for her husband. They might not have gotten married in a human church or court, but their union couldn't be broken by any judge, either.

Noah's chin rested on the top of Hollyn's head and he slowly rocked them side to side.

"I need to go, Noah. I can't stay here," Hollyn whispered as he continued that rocking motion. At her words, he went stock still, his arms tensed around her and he took a step back, still holding her.

"What are you trying to tell me, Hollyn?" he asked. She felt his pain, his confusion, his fear in her heart.

"I can't stay here, Noah. I can't. If they come looking for me—"

"I'll keep you safe. We'll keep you safe," Noah said, his brows pulling low.

"That's what I'm afraid of. If it's just me…" She sighed. "I need to know you're safe. And if I'm here, they're going to come here. What if you get hurt? Or Shawnee? Or even the wolves? There are children there. Micah was right; my presence puts everyone in danger."

Hollyn pulled from his arms and backed away. She felt her magic reaching for him, trying to pull her back into his arms. But she needed space. She needed to think.

"I think that's our decision to make," Carter said.

Hollyn frowned in his direction. "What do you mean?"

"Whether you're a danger to us or not," Carter said.

She'd just thought it and said it, but hearing Carter say it cut her deep. Did they feel the same way Micah did?

"Colton, you have Shawnee," Hollyn said, turning her eyes to Colton. Surely, he'd agree with her.

"I know," he said. Two words. That was it.

"And? Aren't you worried about her?"

"Hollyn—" Noah started, reaching for her, but she backed out of his reach.

"What about your friends in Big River? What about the babies?"

"Enough!" Noah roared, his bear bright in his eyes. Like they had when he'd released on her, his eyes bled back and forth between brown and amber. She'd never seen a Shifter's eyes react like that, never seen someone fight for control over their own body so hard as she had with Noah.

His hands raised to his head and he gripped his short hair tight. He was struggling to remain in his skin. She'd managed to piss off not just her husband, but his bear, as well.

****

Noah continued to tug on his hair, using the sting of his scalp to steady himself. Was Hollyn seriously talking about leaving? She was going to just take off after binding them with her magic? How the fuck did she think that would be possible? How could she think he'd just let her disappear to fight these fuckers alone? How could she even think about leaving Noah? How could she think he'd let her walk away without him?

"Noah," Carter warned, his foot on the first step leading up to his porch. "Come down here, brother. You're too close to Hollyn."

Shit. He was so close to Shifting with Hollyn within feet of him. Even though his bear knew her, would know her no matter what, that didn't mean it was safe for him to explode into his animal near her.

With jerky steps, Noah backed away from Hollyn and climbed down the stairs. His body was vibrating so hard he couldn't see clearly. Couldn't make out the faces of his Clan. Never. In all his years, he'd never been so out of control, so lost to his beast.

Once Noah was far enough from Hollyn to ensure her safety, he turned and looked up at her. She stood, her hands gripping the railing, her eyes wide as she waited. Waited for Noah to calm down, waited for Noah to Shift. Waited for him to let her just walk away. He didn't know, and she probably didn't either. She looked unsure, heartbroken. He pressed the heel of his hand to his chest and realized he couldn't feel her. They'd realized they didn't feel the smaller stuff, like irritation over things like a broken bottle. But with the news she'd received, he should be able to feel her as strongly as he felt his own.

"You're blocking me," he growled out. His mouth became crowded as his teeth Shifted.

Her lips were parted, but she didn't say anything, just watched him closely.

He thought about the agonizing pain he'd felt when Hollyn found out the traffickers might or might not be heading their way. Had she broken their bond?

Searching deep, he still felt her presence, still felt her magic, still felt her heart beating in rhythm with his. She was blocking her emotion from him to help him calm down. It had the opposite effect on his bear. He became panicked, crazed.

"Fuck," Noah muttered, turning his eyes to Carter to warn him to guard Hollyn. Because his bear was intent on marking her permanently. Opening his mouth to warn Carter, Luke, anyone to get Hollyn away from him, his voice was swallowed by the roar of his bear.

Within less than a second, he lost the battle for his skin and looked through the eyes of his bear. He kept trying to push Noah to the back, kept trying to block him, kept trying for full control. And Noah fought just as hard to stay in Bear's head.

Bear turned toward the porch, lifted his head, and released a bellow. Hollyn slapped her hands over her ears. Noah tried to use their connection to warn her, to tell her to run, to get in one of the trucks and head to Big River. Either the connection was truly blocked, or it just didn't work that way.

She didn't run. She didn't even head into the house. She just stood there staring at him with wide eyes, her breath coming in quick pants.

"Noah," Carter said in a calm tone. When Bear didn't even turn his eyes toward the stand-in Alpha, Carter took another step closer. "Bear. You can't have her. You'll hurt her. You could kill her. You could kill your mate."

That stopped Bear. He studied Carter. And then a wave of possessiveness rolled over Noah. Bear thought Carter was trying to take

Hollyn away from him, away from them. *She's our mate. She loves us*, Noah tried to reassure Bear.

Bear took a step in Hollyn's direction until Luke exploded from his skin and blocked his path. He knew his Clan would protect his mate. But now he feared his bear wouldn't stop, he'd just tear through anyone who kept him away from Hollyn.

Colton glanced up at the house as Shawnee stepped out. He held out a hand, telling her to stay back. But Bear wasn't interested in the redhead. *Hollyn. Mate. Mine.*

Luke swiped his massive claw at Bear when he continued his onward trajectory. Bear swung at Luke, challenging him. Noah watched in awe as the most unstable member of their Clan didn't take the bait. He just kept his body between Hollyn and Bear.

"Should I Shift?" Shawnee called from her front porch.

That actually got Bear's attention. He turned his massive head toward her, tilted his head and regarded her. Where Luke kept his cool, Colton, or rather his bear, took the attention as a threat. Colton's bear exploded from his skin.

"For fuck's sake," Carter said, trying to calm the Clan down. "Bear, listen to me. Hollyn is safe. We won't let her run off alone. We'll protect her."

Mine, Bear said. He wanted to be the one to protect her. But first, he needed to make sure she carried his mark. Needed to scar her with his teeth, his claws, he didn't care. As long as her blood carried his scent.

You have to stop, Noah begged. He strained forward, trying to take the reins, trying to push through to take his body back. *This is your Clan. They're trying to protect Hollyn. They're protecting our mate. You can't mark her. You'll hurt her.*

Bear turned back to Hollyn. She'd moved to stand at the top of the stairs. And fear struck Noah hard when she slowly stepped down once, twice, until she was standing on the gravel that was their front yard.

She lifted her chin and closed her eyes. Like a floodgate blasting open, emotions crashed into him, crashed into Bear, making him stumble before righting himself. Her eyes opened and the sapphire was gone; they were as dark as her hair, that onyx color with swirling silver.

Bear released a whine as he watched his mate touch Luke on the shoulder as she passed. She wasn't afraid. She wasn't afraid of the Clan and she wasn't afraid of Bear. Noah, on the other hand was terrified of what Bear would do.

He didn't feel any fear from Hollyn. He felt love. Frustration. Anger. But no fear, not of Bear.

"You already have me, Bear," Hollyn said as she moved closer.

Bear scented the air, raised his head and looked over his shoulder, as if telling her he didn't want her to go.

Hollyn looked in the direction Bear had and slowly shook her head. "It's safer if I go." Her voice was so soft. She jutted her chin out and tried to look confident. But Noah felt her pain at leaving, felt the fear of being alone through their connection.

"We'll keep you safe, Hollyn. I promise," Carter said.

Bear growled at Carter but didn't attack him. He took another step in Hollyn's direction, his lips peeled back to bare his teeth.

"You can *not* bite me, Bear. I'm already yours. I carry your scent. But if you bite me, you could lose me. Do you understand that? Noah, I need you to push through. I need you to stop him."

Bear cocked his head to the side.

"Tell him you'll stay," Shawnee called from her porch. She'd wisely stayed back. She knew her nearness could set Colton off and it would turn into a full-on brawl.

Hollyn glanced up at Shawnee but quickly turned her attention back to Bear. She couldn't risk him taking advantage of her distraction. Smart.

Risking another step closer, Hollyn reached forward, laying her hand on Bear's head when he ducked it to her level. She wasn't a petite woman, but Bear towered over her and could easily hurt her if he wasn't careful.

"You can't mark me, Bear," she reminded him as she stepped closer, raising her other hand to thread her fingers through his fur. "I love you, just as much as I love Noah. I'm already yours. I carry your scent, remember?" She inhaled deeply and smiled softly, just the slightest uptick of her lips. "I'll stay."

A deep rumble came from Bear's chest, the closest thing to a purr he could make. Noah began to calm…until Bear raised his head and opened his mouth. Noah had a direct link to Bear's thoughts. He knew he intended to lick her hand, to show affection, to nuzzle against her.

But his Clan didn't.

Before he could do anything, a blur of fur rammed him from the side, knocking him away from Hollyn. She screamed, but Carter kept her back. Shawnee ran down the stairs, her wide eyes bouncing between Colton and Noah as Luke paced side to side, using his body as a wall to keep Bear away from Hollyn.

"Stop! He wasn't going to hurt me," Hollyn yelled to Colton.

"Sure as hell looked like he was going to bite you," Carter said, his eyes on Noah while holding his arm out to keep Hollyn away. "What the fuck is going on with you Noah?"

"I don't think Noah's in there anymore," Shawnee said from the sidelines. Her eyes glowed a bright gold of her lioness, but she hadn't Shifted yet.

I don't think Noah's in there anymore.

Shit.

Fuck this. He needed his skin back. He'd never been one to lose control and he sure as fuck wasn't going to start today. Hollyn needed him, needed him to be strong, needed him to be in control of himself and his bear.

Forcing the Shift, he groaned in agony as his bear tried to hold on, making the change back to his human form slow and painful. After what felt like a lifetime, he knelt on the ground, the gravel biting into his knees, and panted through the pain.

"He wasn't going to bite her," he said, his voice scratchy and gritty.

"Move," Hollyn said, her voice strained as if she was pushing Carter aside. "I knew he wasn't going to hurt me, dammit," she said, running to his side. She moved to kneel beside him, but he stopped her.

"The gravel hurts," he said and smiled sadly up at her. "He wasn't going to bite you," he repeated.

Pops and grunts sounded behind him. Colton and Luke were Shifting back to their human forms, as well, now that the immediate threat was over.

"I know," Hollyn said, offering Noah a hand and trying to hoist him to his feet. "Are you okay?"

He nodded but tears burned the backs of his eyes. Fuck. He really didn't want to cry in front of his Clan. They'd never let him live it down.

Turning his back on the guys, he shoved his fists against his eyes. "Fuck," he muttered as his throat grew tight.

So many emotions. So much fear. Too much. "Please tell me you'll stay." She'd already made it clear she was doing this to protect all of them, including Noah. That meant she didn't want him to follow. As if that would ever happen. "Please," he begged on a whisper.

Hollyn's hands trembled as she raised them and cupped his face. "I'll stay," she whispered back.

The tears fell freely now. He couldn't have stopped them to save his life. Relief. Immense relief poured through him and Hollyn smiled just before she rose onto her tiptoes and pressed a kiss to his cheek. She used her thumbs to wipe away the tears that trailed down his cheek, but she was crying now, too.

Noah laughed through the tears, wiping hers away like she was doing his. "We're a fucking mess."

Hollyn chuckled, too, then wrapped her arms around his waist, pressing her cheek against his chest.

He held her tight, maybe too tight. But she didn't protest. And he couldn't make himself release her. He didn't care that his dick was flopping in the wind or that his Clan were making themselves scarce while Noah and Hollyn had their moment. All he cared about was the woman in his arms. Two weeks and she'd become the most precious and important thing in the world to him. He loved his Clan, loved his friends, but he'd run with her as far as she wanted if she'd let him. He'd spend every second of every day keeping her safe and making her happy.

His bear rumbled contentedly in his head. Maybe he didn't get to mark their mate, but she'd promised to stay with them. She'd told Bear she loved him, reminded him she carried her scent. They would probably have to cover her more than once a week, but she hadn't seemed to mind. And since he got to feel the pleasure, too, he sure as hell wasn't going to protest.

"We're going to be late," Shawnee called from her front door. She didn't sound like her usual chipper self this morning. Nope. She was pissed, and probably at Noah.

She of all people should know how crazy their animals could go over their mates.

"Shit," Noah muttered. He'd destroyed the clothes he'd been wearing. "You still up for working today?" he asked. Now that she was no longer blocking him, he could feel not only the emotions she'd had over the discovery of the traffickers' movement and Noah's bear freaking out, but the nausea and headache of her hangover.

"I go where you go," she said, smiling through her tears. Noah pulled her back into his arms and buried his face in her hair.

I go where you go. At least now he knew she wouldn't block him and run away. She would let him be by her side, let him fight this fight with her, if that's what it came to. She trusted him, trusted him to keep her safe. She loved him, loved his animal half.

This woman who spent her whole life fearing Shifters was his mate, accepted his bear as her mate. This woman was *more* than a mate. This woman was his wife. Thick and thin and all that shit. He loved her more than he knew was physically possible. He loved her more than he ever loved anyone. His bear hummed in approval in his head as he pulled her scent deep inside of him and vowed to burn down the fucking planet to keep her out of the hands of anyone who would hurt her.

Chapter Nine

It had been three days since they'd gotten word that the traffickers were on the move. Of course, Hollyn was still on edge, but a certain kind of peace had overcome her after Noah's bear burst forward. She couldn't explain it. It was almost like she was drawing strength from her connection, or maybe she was feeling Bear's emotions as well as Noah's. Bear had no doubt he'd keep Hollyn safe, whereas Noah was constantly paranoid. He always made sure every window and door was locked and the curtains were pulled closed every night. He'd explained about how Shawnee's family Pack had attempted to sneak up on Colton and Shawnee, but he rarely fell asleep right away because of his work schedule. They hadn't planned on anyone being awake.

All Hollyn knew was the Clan tended to congregate on Noah's porch any time the two of them were home. And they came in for lunch with the wolves from Big River every single day. Except the women. They'd been staying away, keeping the babies away.

The guilt of staying there when she knew how dangerous her presence could be was a constant for her. And since Noah could feel it, he reassured her over and over everyone wanted her there, not just him.

"Why don't you take a break and eat something," Noah said.

"Why?" she asked. The lunch rush was over and the room had cleared of all but the regulars who stayed glued to their seats until it was time to stumble out to their ride.

"Because you've been working your ass off nonstop for the last three days. Go. Eat something." Noah frowned when Hollyn crossed her arms and raised her brows to her hairline. "Why do I have to go through this with every employee. You're allowed to take a break, Hollyn. Just because you're mated to the owner doesn't mean you're married to the bar."

He turned her by her shoulders and swatted her on the ass to get her moving. She couldn't help the girly giggle that burst through her lips. Not only had he become almost militant in the way he checked the house before letting her in, always scanning the area when they got in and out of the car, locking up every night, but he'd become almost insatiable in the bedroom. She wasn't complaining.

Bear had to cover her in his scent again the night he'd freaked out. It was like he was reassuring himself that everyone knew she was claimed. She'd never thought she was the kind of woman who would like that kind of mentality, the whole cave man thing, the whole claiming thing. But…Noah was hers, too. She'd marked him with her magic. Her flames flowed through his veins, letting anyone with the same gifts know he belonged to her.

Hollyn veered into the kitchen and fixed herself something to eat. Without asking, she fixed an order for Shawnee, too. She didn't even have to ask; the woman ate the same thing every day: burger with a side of sweet potato fries.

She carried the two baskets out and jerked her head for Shawnee to join her. Ever since Bear had taken over Noah's body, Shawnee had treated Noah differently. She wasn't mean, per se, but she wasn't as sweet and cheerful as she was when Hollyn first came to Blackwater. It had to stop. Now.

Once Shawnee was situated with a glass of soda and had taken a big bite of her burger, Hollyn leaned forward on her elbows and kept her voice as soft as possible. "What's going on with you and Noah?"

Shawnee's eyes jerked to Hollyn's face and she swallowed audibly. Turning to look at their boss over her shoulder, Shawnee turned back around, a deep crease between her brows. "He shouldn't have done that," she said and took a huge, aggressive bite of her burger.

It was Hollyn's turn to frown. "Done what?" Noah hadn't done anything to Shawnee as far as she knew.

"Gone all furry and crap. He could've really hurt you, Hollyn. We're not like that. He's supposed to protect you. That's what real mates do. They don't get all crazy and let their bear—"

Hollyn held her hand up. "He didn't hurt me, though. And I knew he wouldn't. Our situation is a little different. Remember the story you told me about your lioness finally coming out when your mate was in trouble?" Shawnee nodded as she slipped a fry between her lips. "Well, his bear can't even mark his mate. And…we still don't know if I'm at risk or not. How do you think Colton's bear would've reacted if he couldn't mark you as his? Was he super calm when your family Pride showed up?"

Shawnee's eyes left Hollyn's face and she looked around the room as if watching the memory play out in the middle of Moe's. Slowly, her head began to wag side to side.

"Still," Shawnee said, looking back at Noah again. Either he couldn't hear them or was pretending not to because he seemed oblivious to their conversation.

When Shawnee turned back around, a little of the anger had left her eyes. After learning more about Shawnee's past, Hollyn understood. But like she'd said, they were a unique case. Even if she'd been human Noah could've marked her. He would've risked turning her, of course, but she'd have a much better chance at survival than Hollyn.

Hollyn finished eating before Shawnee but she hung out with her, chatting about nothing in particular. The last three days had been intense; she just wanted her life to go back to the way it was two weeks ago. Back when she was building a future with Noah, back when she was getting to know everyone, back when she thought she'd finally be free and safe.

"We should have a girl's day," Hollyn announced. She wasn't sure it would happen or if any of the guys would let any of their mates out of their sights, but they could always have it right there at Moe's. Dance to the music, drink a little, and just enjoy their time together.

"Yes! Definitely," Shawnee said, pulling her phone from her back pocket to text all the girls.

Hollyn still didn't have a phone. And that was fine with her. She was always with Noah, anyway, so she could use his phone if she needed to contact someone. Besides, the only people she really cared to talk to were the same people he'd brought into her life.

"Nova's in," Shawnee announced, then smiled when her phone dinged a few more times. "They're all in."

"Who's in what?" Noah asked as he neared the table. He bent and pressed a kiss to Hollyn's forehead. That was something else she'd noticed; his need to touch her had grown, too.

"Girl's night," Hollyn said, turning a wide grin on Noah as she prepared for his argument. She didn't have to wait long.

"Have it here," he said as a muscle ticked in his jaw.

"That's what I was thinking," Hollyn said.

"But we're here every day," Shawnee whined. "Can't we have one night without all you stinky boys?"

"No matter where you go there will be stinky boys. And I'm not comfortable with Hollyn out there alone. Not without knowing where the pricks are."

"She wouldn't be alone," Shawnee said. "My lioness is strong. So is Nova's wolf. And Cujo would never let anything happen to her."

Noah pinched the bridge of his nose. "How about we contact Colton and the rest of the guys and see what they think," Noah said and smirked when Shawnee crossed her arms and stuck out her bottom lip.

"I'll block off the section in the back. It'll be your little private party," Noah said.

Hollyn didn't really care if they had privacy or not. Really, she just wanted to be with her friends, and she wanted to make sure they still cared about her. The rational part of her brain assured her they did, indeed, still care, but were trying to keep the cubs safe. The more women who stayed home while the men were at work, the safer the baby girls were. But the irrational part of her was scared she'd once again be alone and without a family.

She'd always have Noah, though. She'd promised him she wouldn't leave, that she'd stay with him no matter what.

"Who's going to wait the tables?" Shawnee asked. If they had a little party, Noah would be working the bar by himself.

"I ran this place on my own for years before you two came along. I'll be fine," Noah's eyes dropped to Hollyn. Something flashed through them, something she couldn't identify, but she felt a rush of anger go through her before it faded. Surely, Noah wasn't angry that she wanted some alone time with her female friends.

Noah bent at the waist and sipped at her lips once, twice, before straightening and heading back behind the bar. He began to restock the coolers for the dinner rush, his gaze finding her occasionally in the mirror hanging over the selection of liquor as if he were reassuring himself Hollyn was still there and safe. And he was probably comforting his bear at the same time.

"Guess we should get back to work," Hollyn said, bending her back over the chair to stretch. It'd taken a while for her body to get used to the constant work again, but damn it felt good. She'd missed it. She'd missed the modicum of independence.

"Yep," Shawnee said, slowly pushing from her seat.

The bar would fill with the dinner crowd soon. They needed to get the tables cleaned up, the condiments filled, and prep the kitchen.

And then, in a blink of an eye, another day was gone. It seemed the older Hollyn got, the faster her days passed. She could remember as a young teenager thinking eighteen was so far away. Then twenty-one. Now, in a few years, she'd hit forty. Time sure did fly. It felt like the first half of her life had been wasted, like she'd just survived, just existed before Noah and the bear Clan. Before Aron and the panthers. Before she'd learned she could trust someone else. Before she'd learned she could trust a Shifter. Before she'd learned she could love a Shifter.

Just like every night the past three nights, the three bears of Blackwater waited for Noah, Hollyn, and Shawnee to get off work. And, just like the past three nights, the four guys went out first, letting Hollyn and Shawnee follow them out when they were positive there was no one waiting for them.

The second Hollyn stepped through the door, the sensation of an oncoming storm rolled over her skin again, just like it had a week ago. Static electricity made the hair on her arms stand on end and sent a shiver down her spine. But, just like that night, there wasn't a single cloud in the Autumn evening sky. Maybe it was the cool air that made her shiver. But that didn't explain the electric shock feeling, didn't explain her hair standing up as if she'd rubbed a balloon on her arm.

"What's wrong?" Noah asked when he noticed she wasn't moving toward the vehicle. His eyes flashed to amber immediately and he looked around, his nostrils flaring as he scented the air for a threat.

She looked around, sent her magic further than her eyes and ears could detect, seeking the source of the sensation clinging to her like a cloak. Nothing. She couldn't feel anyone nearby, couldn't find the source. "Nothing. I don't know."

"You look scared," Shawnee said, narrowing her eyes at Hollyn.

The other three Clan brothers moved to stand closer to her, ready to block anyone from getting to her.

"Seriously. It's nothing. I just thought I felt…something."

"Can your magic warn you if someone's in the area?" Carter asked.

"Only within a certain distance. If it can't reach it, then I won't feel it." She only had about a five yard radius to which her magic could roam. After that, she was blind.

Luke moved away from Hollyn, his head tilted back, his nostrils flaring the way Noah's did. His eyes were glowing now, too, ready for battle with an unseen enemy. His boots crunched in the gravel, the sound so loud in the quiet night. There were no cars driving past, no other businesses open this late. It was just them.

"It's nothing. Sorry. Didn't mean to freak everyone out," Hollyn said, trying to sound as calm as possible, but there was something about that sensation, something familiar. She just couldn't put her finger on it, couldn't pluck the memory from her brain.

"Can you describe it? What did you feel?" Carter asked.

Hollyn looked up at Noah. His teeth were clenched so tight Hollyn wondered if he'd have any molars left by the time all this was over. With a shrug, she turned back to Carter. "Like that feeling you get during a lightning storm. I don't know if you guys can feel it as strongly as I can, but whenever a storm is close by, it feels like a big cloud of static electricity around me." She rubbed her arm as she spoke, pressing the hair back down.

"Do you still feel it?" Shawnee asked.

Yeah. She did. But since she couldn't find anything and they didn't detect anyone, there was no reason to rile up the whole Clan.

"Nah. It was nothing. Probably just a chill from the wind."

"Wind doesn't make the hair on your arms stand up," Luke said, his eyes glued to where she tried to smooth the hair back into place.

Hollyn dropped her hand and shook her head. "Let's just go home. I'm tired."

Noah studied her face a few seconds before nodding. He took her hand in his and led her to the truck. Colton and Shawnee rode home with them while Carter and Luke followed close behind. Seriously. They were so close Hollyn couldn't see Luke's headlight in the side mirror. She just hoped Noah didn't have to stop short for a deer, because Luke was going to end up smashing into their bumper.

****

Hollyn could pretend she was fine all she wanted, but Noah had a direct link to the fear burning a path through her veins. He could feel her racing heart, feel the adrenaline coursing through her system. She might not know what had caused the sensation, but she was scared of it.

Once everyone was in their own cabins, Noah turned to Hollyn. "Tell me," he said, biting back the growl of his bear. He hated how little control he had over his bear since Hollyn had come into his life.

"What?" she asked, toeing her shoes off at the entrance. Ever since that first day when Hollyn and Shawnee had straightened up his cabin, he'd made a conscious effort to keep it that way. Including removing his shoes at the doorway. It was something Hollyn did every time and the habit wore off on him.

Noah followed Hollyn down the hall to the bathroom. She pulled off her clothes and turned a sly smile on him. He knew exactly what she was doing; she was trying to distract him from his questions. She knew he'd felt her terror, her nerves back at Moe's.

And as much as he'd love nothing more than to have his hands on his beautiful mate, he needed to know if they needed to call the panthers in as backup. He'd call in every single fucking Shifter he knew to keep Hollyn safe.

Noah let his eyes roam her body from her strong thighs to her soft belly, her wide hips, to her small waist then up to her perky tits. Fuck, he loved looking at her. He loved touching her more. But he had to squash his libido for now, at least until he knew what kind of threat they were facing. For some reason, the fear she'd felt when she stepped outside was stronger and different than the fear she had of the traffickers.

"What was that back at the bar? For a second, you looked like you expected someone to appear out of thin air," Noah said, crossing his arms over his chest to keep them for reaching for her.

When Hollyn realized Noah wasn't falling for her little seduction act, she covered herself with her arms and turned to start the shower. Neither of them could stand to go to bed with the cigarette smoke in their hair and clinging to their skin.

"I don't know." She glanced at Noah over her shoulder. He stood with his arms still crossed and one brow cocked. "Seriously, Noah. I mean…it felt familiar, but I can't place it. Whatever it was wasn't comfortable."

"Explain," he said, finally pulling his own clothes off to join her. It was quicker for them to shower together so they could get to bed faster. At least it was on the nights they didn't get carried away and ended up making love under the spray.

Noah stepped into the shower behind Hollyn and reached over her shoulder for his soap. Hollyn liked all the girly smelling shit where he just wanted to be clean. A bar of good old-fashioned Ivory was fine with him.

"I can't. That's the problem. It kind of…" She went quiet as she rubbed the soapy puffy thing on her arm. "It felt like magic, but not fire magic. Like I said, it felt familiar, but I just can't place it."

"Another Fairy?"

She turned and let the water sluice over her hair, her face, her shoulders until it dripped off her erect pink nipples. And Noah was suddenly having a hard time focusing on the conversation.

Her slender shoulders rose and fell as she stepped out of the spray, giving Noah a chance to rinse off as she squeezed the water from her hair. "I mean, I guess it could've been. But why did I feel it so strongly? Wouldn't that mean they were close by? Did they not want me to see them or something?"

"Would another Fairy be a threat to you?"

"I wouldn't think so. We pretty much stay hidden. You'd think if it was another Fairy, he'd want an ally. But you guys were with me. Maybe he was scared of you."

That sounded feasible enough. According to Hollyn, the Fae were terrified of Shifters, and history had given them plenty of reasons as to why. The newcomer would have no reason to believe he'd be safe with the bears. Although, if they'd been paying close enough attention, they would've seen the Clan was protecting Hollyn, not holding her captive.

Noah tilted his head back to rinse the shampoo. When he lowered it, his eyes immediately found Hollyn, and her eyes were on his junk. Yeah. He was hard. He was hard any time he saw his mate naked. He literally had no control over his body when it came to her.

Hollyn slowly looked up at Noah through her lashes. "You know, I can help you with that," she teased, reaching behind him to shut off the water.

With water still trailing down her body, she reached forward and wrapped her hand around his shaft, taking a long, slow pull on it. Noah hissed through his teeth and bucked into her hand. She could drive him crazy with a simple touch. Stepping closer, she kept her hand wrapped around him, stroking him slowly, and moved into his space, pressing her tits against his chest. He loved that. He loved the feeling of her softness against him.

Hollyn tilted her head back, her gaze dropping to his mouth. She raised onto her toes, but Noah bent forward before she moved too much and slipped on the slick tub. At first, the kiss was sensual and soft. And then it turned hurried and hungry, her hand moving on him faster.

His balls tightened and Noah jerked away from her. No way. He was not finishing without her. Not that he wouldn't have taken care of her after, but he loved the way she felt clenching around his dick, the way her orgasm milked his own from him.

Gripping her hands in his, he threaded his fingers through hers and gently put them behind her back, caging him in his arms. She was at his mercy. His bear paced impatiently in his head. He'd already covered her in his scent three days ago, but with possible threats coming at them constantly, he felt the need to make sure everyone knew she was claimed. And since he couldn't mark her, this was the only way to keep him from losing his shit and hurting Hollyn.

"Hi, Bear," Hollyn said in a husky voice as she looked up into Noah's eyes.

Oh, Noah was fully present. There was no doubt about that. But Bear was fully aware of everything going on and was ready to feel their mate in their hands.

Noah smiled as he took Hollyn's lips again, releasing her hands so he could wrap his arms around her back and pull her even closer, if that was at all possible. He loved this woman. He loved that she accepted both sides of him, loved that she trusted him, trusted his bear.

Lifting her into his arms, he smiled against her lips when she instinctively wrapped her legs around his waist. He stepped out of the tub, holding her tight against him, and carried her to the sink. No way could he make it to the bed; he was too close, too far gone.

The second the cool sink hit Hollyn's ass, she reached between them and guided him to her core. She was warm and wet and ready for him. Noah slid in with ease and gritted his teeth as she squeezed around him, the delicious resistance pushing him even closer. Maybe this was a bad idea. He needed to work her some more, because with her wrapped around him, her tongue plunging into his mouth, her tits pressed up against him, he was about to blow his load.

And then reality hit him. Fuck. Condom.

When Noah pulled from her fully, she groaned her frustration and pulled her mouth away to frown up at him.

"Condom," he growled out. Why was he already so fucking breathless?

Hollyn shifted to lower to her feet, but Noah had to take advantage of her at this height. As he lowered to his knees, her sex was lined up perfectly with his mouth. Hollyn smiled a lusty smile and leaned against the wall, her head touching the mirror. She threaded her fingers through his hair and urged him closer.

A surprised gasp tore from her lips when he gave her folds a long, slow lick then nipped at her swollen clit. Already he knew her body, knew what she liked, knew how she liked it. But he still loved to find new ways to make her squirm and moan.

Gripping her thighs in his hands, he pushed them further apart and toward her chest, opening her for him fully. He teased her clit, dipped his tongue inside, even teased at her back door. She didn't seem to like that. He chuckled against her when she grunted and simply said, "Uh uh."

Noah nipped at her thighs, making her squirm, then dove face first into bliss. He licked and sucked on her clit until her breathing changed and her muscles in her thighs tightened. She crested with his name on her lips, and, just as her aftershocks slowed, he stood and plunged to the hilt inside her heat.

He stayed there, relishing the way her walls clamped and released on him as the last of her orgasm made her twitch, and then he began to pump into her. There was no slow and sensual. Hell no. He pounded into her, determined to pull another orgasm from her before he found his own release. And it didn't take long.

"Oh! Oh my…Noah!" she screamed as another wave gripped her even before the first faded away. She sat up and clutched at his arms, her tits bouncing against him. And that was all he could handle.

Noah pulled from her and trapped his dick between them, spilling on her stomach, on his, and gritted his teeth, moaning as each wave hit him. They'd never made it to the bedroom, never donned a condom, but at least he'd had a working brain cell left and he made sure to pull from her.

He only stepped away enough to grab a washcloth and wet it in the sink behind Hollyn's irresistible ass. He grabbed a handful before bringing the washcloth back around to clean them both off. They were covered in a sheen of sweat, but they could always take a quick shower in the morning. For now, he was whipped. And he knew she had to be, too.

His woman worked as hard as him, ensuring he had a partner in the bar, making sure he took breaks to sit with his friends while she took over the drinks. He loved to watch her interact with the customers, loved the wide grin she got after performing a trick and getting loud praise from the entire room. Loved her.

Once his mate was clean, Noah scooped her into his arms and carried her from the bathroom, using his elbow to flip off the light. His bear was rumbling with contentment. Although Noah hadn't intentionally covered Hollyn in his scent – it was a last minute thought since he'd never retrieved a condom – his bear loved that she'd carry it for day.

Or until the next time Bear grew possessive.

Chapter Ten

Ever since they'd left Moe's a week ago, Hollyn couldn't shake the feeling of static clinging to her skin. The only time she didn't notice it was when Noah had her so out of her mind with lust, the world could've burned down around them and she would've been oblivious. But times like this, when the bar was slow, when there was nothing to do, when there was no one waving her over or begging her to show them another trick, she was uneasy. And she knew Noah felt it.

She'd attempted to block him from her emotion, to shield him in a way, but it'd just made Bear frantic. He'd panicked and almost caused a fight within his own Clan. Luke was uber protective of Hollyn and Shawnee, of any female really. And he'd been hanging out on their porch a lot. In fact, he'd been there each time she'd woken up in the morning. Surely, he wasn't sleeping out there every night.

Even with the extra layer of protection, she constantly felt like there were eyes on her, yet there was never anyone around. Even the bears couldn't pick up the scent. It was creepy and made her wonder if she was paranoid from so many years of running.

"You almost ready?" Shawnee asked her. It was their official girl's night out, and, just like Noah had mentioned, the guys weren't hip on the idea of all the women out alone when they had no idea where the traffickers were.

It wasn't that the guys didn't think they could take care of themselves; Hollyn figured it was the fact they could get hurt or worse trying to protect Hollyn. That just made the guilt she'd been carrying for a few weeks grow.

"Yep. Let me close out my drawer," Hollyn said.

"Go. I got it," Noah said. Being as it was only the two of them who used the register, there was no reason he couldn't take over. As she turned and pressed a peck to his cheek, all the women from Big River piled through the door.

"Party time, bitches," Nova called out, her arms in the air. "Dad's babysitting both girls tonight, so I'm going to have some fun."

Callie smiled at Noah and Hollyn. "The guys said they'd pick us up tonight," she said, as if letting them know they had a designated driver. Even if they hadn't, Hollyn and Noah would've made sure they got home safely.

Hollyn watched as they filed in, each one looking like they were going out on a night in downtown St. Louis instead of another night at the same bar they frequented regularly. Nova wore a pair of skinny jeans that hugged her curves and a top that strategically hung off one shoulder, making Hollyn a little jealous of her full hips and boobs. Callie wore a pair of boot leg jeans and a sparkly tank top that dipped a little low in the front. Lola wore a cute t-shirt with a pastel unicorn across the front and a leather mini skirt. Peyton's bleached white hair was pulled up into a knot, showing off all the purple streaks underneath. She wore a skin tight, cut way up to there mini skirt and knee-high boots. Emory, well, Emory dressed the way she always did, a pair of jeans and a t-shirt, but the ensemble just looked perfect on her.

Looking down at herself, Hollyn wondered if she should've brought a change of clothes with her. Oh, who was she kidding? She worked here all day. Why would she dress up for the place now? Besides, her usual work outfit was flashy enough as it was.

"Shots!" Nova yelled, then started to rap. "Shots shots, shotsshotsshots." And that was apparently all the words she knew to that song. It didn't matter. Her level of excitement was contagious. Before long, Hollyn was retrieving tray after tray of shots, nothing fancy, just straight up Jager shots, or Wild Honey, or whatever Noah decided to pour.

Emory jogged over to the jukebox and skimmed through the selection. "Noah, can I change the music?" He held up the remote, making sure she saw it since she'd already had a few, then tossed it to her. One after another, Emory made sure every song was a dancing song. And then she dragged the women onto the floor.

Callie was a little timid at first, barely moving, just sort of swaying. But Nova, she went all out, swinging her hair, lip syncing to songs and pretending she held a microphone and would hold it front of one of the other girls to sing.

Eventually, they were all bouncing around like fools and Hollyn laughed until she could barley breathe. "I've got to sit down. I'm burning up," Hollyn yelled over the music.

"Shifter hearing." Nova pointed to her ear. "No reason to yell, Tinkerbell," Nova yelled and then froze.

Hollyn's eyes immediately found Noah who was glaring at Nova. But if anyone else heard Nova's nickname for Hollyn, they either didn't notice or didn't understand. They probably just figured it was another drunk chick being silly.

Hollyn turned back to Nova with wide eyes and shook her head.

Sorry, Nova mouthed.

That was what she'd been afraid of, what Noah had been afraid of, someone slipping in front of the wrong people.

On shaky legs, Hollyn made her way to the bar for some water. After her last hangover, she wanted to do everything she could to avoid another. And that included slowing down and staying hydrated. She downed the first glass and grabbed the spray to refill her cup.

"You doing okay?" Noah asked, his eyes narrowed at Nova for a second before turning to Hollyn.

"Yeah. Just hot." And the alcohol was helping quash the staticky, pins and needles feeling on his skin.

"Better slow down or we'll both be hurting tomorrow," Noah said with a deep chuckle. She loved that sound. She loved when he let his guard down at work and was the sweet, sexy guy she knew at home. He'd also just given her a reminder of his direct link to everything she was feeling. Guilt. It felt like that had been her running emotion since day one.

As the girls continued to dance and laugh, she pushed that stupid guilt aside. These were her people. She shouldn't feel guilty that they wanted to keep her safe. She'd do the same thing for every single one of them.

Downing her second glass of water, she handed it to Noah and jogged back to the girls. Maybe she'd just sweat some of the alcohol out of her system. Either way, she wasn't done having fun, not yet. She deserved a night to let loose. They all did.

Every time Hollyn looked up at Noah, he was watching her. Whether he was pouring a drink, talking to a customer, or just leaning against the bar, his eyes were on Hollyn. There was hunger and lust there, no doubt, but there was so much more. As she sought out that thread that bound them, she could feel his love, she could feel his affection, but she could also feel his fear and worry. This was the first time Hollyn wished he didn't work at Moe's, didn't own the place, because it would be so nice to pull him out onto the floor and dance with him, just enjoy each other and pretend nothing else was outside that door.

Hollyn raised her hand and gave Noah a finger wave with a huge grin. And then she opened the connection wide and let him feel everything, the way her heart beat to his rhythm, the way her soul cradled his, the way she couldn't wait until they were home alone.

His slow smile was crooked and sexy and full of promises. He sent her a wink and turned to take another drink order.

"Where's the pretty girl with the fire?" a woman called out to Noah.

He didn't raise his eyes to Hollyn, didn't tip the woman off that the pretty girl was in the same room. "She's off tonight."

"Well damn. What night is she working this week?" she asked, one hand on her hip. She turned to scan the room and Hollyn ducked behind Nova and Emory to hide from her sight. The last thing she needed was to be talked into performing when she was inebriated.

Hollyn scratched and rubbed at her arm as the woman turned back to Noah who was staring down at her with a scowl etched deep in the lines of his face.

"Don't know if she's coming back," he said.

The old codger who sat at the bar all day, John, turned to face the newcomer. "Heard she moved to another state. Something about a big job opportunity."

Okay. All that wasn't necessary. Hollyn wanted to avoid being conned into working during girls' night, not run off a customer.

The woman turned to John, pushing her dark hair over her shoulder, and stared at him for a few seconds. "You sure about that?"

John leaned away from her, his eyes going to Noah.

"She ain't here. Don't know if she'll come back. You want a drink?" Noah said in that gruff tone he used with his customers.

The woman glanced over her shoulder toward the tables and in Hollyn's direction, but she stayed hidden behind her friends. *Just go*, she mentally begged the woman as she once again rubbed her hands against her arms.

With a huff of breath as if she were so put out, the woman shrugged. "Guess I'll have to catch the show another time." She lifted her hand in a short wave to Noah and stepped through the door.

Hollyn finally stepped out from behind the girls and smiled at Noah as she shook her head. He nodded once, bent to John and it looked like he'd said *thanks* and handed John another beer. Hollyn a had a feeling that one was on the house.

Throwing her arms over her head, Hollyn went back to dancing and acting like a fool with her friends until closing time rolled around. Her feet ached, she was covered in sweat, but damn she'd had fun.

All the guys from Big River, Eli, and her Clan brothers piled through the door just in time for last call. They weren't there to drink; they were there to get their drunk mates home and to make sure Noah and Hollyn were okay when they left.

"That was so much fun," Callie said, dipping under Micah's arm to press against his side. "You guys should've totally come earlier and danced with us."

"I wanted to come get jiggy with it, but Lola told me we were forbidden," Reed pouted, pressing a kiss to Lola's temple.

"Did you behave?" Gray asked Nova as she pulled her purse strap over her shoulder.

"Believe it or not, I did," Nova said with a wink.

"No problems?" Carter asked Noah.

"Nah. It was a little on the slow side, so they pretty much had free run of the place," Noah said as he began wiping down the bar top and washing glasses.

Well, shit. Hollyn couldn't just stand there and watch him work. If she helped, they'd get out of there quicker. And just like on the nights when Hollyn and Shawnee worked, the others jumped in to help them get all their closing crap done faster.

"Hollyn has a fan," Nova said, tilting her head to look up at Gray.

"Oh yeah?" Gray asked, raising one brow at Noah. He assumed it was a male.

"Not like that," Nova said, putting her hand on his cheek and turning his face toward her. "This chick showed up and asked for the pretty girl with the tricks."

"The fire," Hollyn said as she put away the clean glasses.

"Huh?" Nova said.

Did Hollyn look as drunk as Nova? She didn't feel that drunk. Definitely not as bad as her first night at Big River when she'd told everyone her secret.

"She asked for the girl with the fire," Hollyn said.

"The *pretty* girl," Nova added. "You think she has a crush on you?"

"Really? That's the first place your mind goes?" Hollyn asked. They were done behind the bar and the rest of the group had already wiped down the tables, stacked the chairs, and swept and mopped the floor. There wasn't much else to be done.

"Of course it does. I told you she's a perv. All her books are about sex," Emory said.

"Romance," Tristan, the super quiet guy from Big River, said as he stood with his arm around Peyton's shoulders.

"Yeah, yeah. Romance, too. But a lot of sex," Emory said, her eyes wide.

Hollyn chuckled as she followed everyone out the door and waited as Noah locked the door.

"Why would she ask for the girl with fire?" Micah asked. "Why'd she phrase it like that?"

"'Cause I blow flames?" Hollyn said with a shrug.

"She didn't say the girl who blew flames. She asked for the pretty girl with the fire," Noah said as he turned back from the door.

Hollyn rubbed at her arms and shrugged again. "No idea."

"Do you have a rash or something?" Micah asked, his intense gaze where Hollyn was rubbing nonstop.

"No. It's just that…" Hollyn was going to explain it was that weird staticky feeling, tell them it felt like when your foot falls asleep.

And then puzzle pieces began to slam into place one after the other. "The girl with the fire," she muttered.

The woman hadn't asked for the girl who did tricks, didn't say she blew flames, she'd asked for the girl with the fire. And the pins and needles sensation had escalated with her presence and had barely faded since she left. Was that woman a Fairy? Had she been in the presence of another Fae woman and run her off?

But…

If she was Fae, wouldn't she have been more careful with her wording? She wouldn't have wanted to out Hollyn, especially if she knew Hollyn was an Elemental Fae with the gift of fire. And why was she there to begin with? Why was she looking for Hollyn? In general, Fae tended to steer pretty clear of each other. They were too damn endangered to risk being in the same place at the same time. Someone could easily snatch or kill both of them and that would be two less Fae on the planet.

"Are you going to be sick?" Nova asked. "You just went super pale."

"She was Fae," Hollyn said, flicking her eyes up to Noah before searching the area.

"Who?" Nova asked, oblivious in her boozed up state.

"That woman, the lady who asked for me. She was Fae. That's who I've been feeling this whole time. I just…it's been so many years since I felt another Fae's presence, I'd forgotten about it." Hollyn rubbed her hands up and down her arms some more. If the lady was gone, why did she still feel her magic? Was that normal? Did it cling to people? She didn't know and had no one to ask.

Big River tensed and guided their mates to their waiting trucks. "Oh, for fuck's sake," Peyton said, pulling her arm from Tristan's grasp. "I can take on every single one of you and you know it. Don't treat me like I'm fragile. I'm staying until she gets in her truck," Peyton said, jerking her chin toward Hollyn. "It's either that or Cujo is going to lose her shit."

It was definitely time to go. Until she knew what the woman's motives were for tracking Hollyn down, she wanted to keep a good distance between them. And since she had no idea whether the woman's magic was clinging to her or if she was still close, watching them from the shadows, blocking the Shifters from being able to scent her, she didn't want to stand there exposed.

Hollyn slipped her hand into Noah's and winced when his grip was a little too tight. "Ease up there, big boy," she said, smiling up at him in hopes of easing the anger now burning bright in his amber eyes.

It didn't matter how wide she grinned or how much she teased him; he could feel her fear burning hot in her veins.

****

Noah laid on his side, raised up on his elbow, his head propped in his hand, and watched Hollyn sleep. He'd barely gotten more than a few hours and that had only been thirty minutes here and fifteen minutes there. He couldn't sleep, especially with his bear pacing and growling in his head.

He'd started doing that when Noah had felt the fear coming from Hollyn like a punch in the gut. It took everything in him and a lot of bartering and negotiating to keep his skin. His bear wanted out. He wanted to track down the person sniffing around his mate and destroy her.

But that wouldn't happen. For one thing, they had no idea if this woman was friend or foe. Two, she was a Fairy; no way would he be a part of their elimination on this planet. And three…Noah couldn't hurt a woman. He just couldn't. Even when Tammen and Deathport had attacked Big River, he couldn't fight back against the lioness. And when Shawnee's former Pride attacked, he again couldn't fight back against the females. He'd taken so many lashes and bites, but he never once struck back.

Hollyn sighed in her sleep and rolled onto her side. A few minutes later, her lashes fluttered and her eyes opened.

"Are you watching me sleep?" she asked, closing her eyes and folding her hands beneath her face.

He grunted.

When her eyes opened again, she kept them on Noah. "You're still worried about last night," she said, as her magic flowed between them. Again, he just grunted and dipped his head once.

Hollyn rolled onto her back and lifted her arms over her head, her palms going flat against the headboard as she stretched. The movement made the blanket slide down and reveal one of her perfect tits. He couldn't help himself; he reached one hand forward and cupped it, tweaking her nipple between his finger and thumb once before pulling his hand back.

She rolled her head to look at him with a soft, sleepy smile. "I figured you'd be tired after last night."

In Noah's frantic, freaked out state, his bear's possessive need, and Hollyn's drunken horniness, they'd screwed on just about every piece of furniture Noah owned. He was tired, but it wasn't from making love to his mate.

His face softened the same time his dick hardened as she dragged the blanket lower, revealing her other boob. He wanted her. Then again, he always wanted her. But they had some things to discuss first.

"Did you recognize that woman?" he asked.

Disappointment was evident in her face the same time it hit him in the chest. She covered back up and shook her head on the pillow. "No. Never seen her before."

Noah grabbed the blanket and pulled it back down. Just because they had to talk didn't mean he couldn't have the perfect view during the conversation. She smiled up at him, her eyes sleepy as she shook her head.

"I don't think I want you at the bar for a while," Noah said.

"I thought we already discussed it was the safest place for me," she said, pushing up onto her elbows.

As her boobs swayed and jiggled, Noah almost lost his train of thought.

"I put in a call with Aron. He's sending Brax and Daxon to hang out for a while. They'll be here tomorrow."

"You called a babysitter," she said, sitting all the way up and pulling the blanket all the way to her damn chin. She was cutting off his view of her body as punishment.

"I called in backup," he said, pushing up to a sitting position. He didn't bother to cover up as he climbed from the bed. They had two hours before they had to be at work. He decided to hold off on the shower until after they'd hashed all this out. Pulling on a pair of sweats, he sat on the edge of the bed and pushed some hair away from Hollyn's face. "Just until we figure out who that woman is. And where the traffickers are. And until the whole fucking deal is over."

"So…forever," she said, narrowing her eyes on him as she leaned her back against the headboard. "I'm a hot commodity, Big Boy. There will always be someone out there searching for someone like me. It'll never be over. You sure you want to deal with that for the rest of your life? You sure you want to constantly feel the pain and fear I feel every single fucking time something like this happens?"

He hated every emotion flowing from Hollyn into Noah. He hated that she doubted his commitment to her. And he flinched a little at her use of the F word. It was the first time he'd ever heard her drop that bomb. If everything else she'd said hadn't pissed him off, he might've actually smiled at how cute it sounded coming from her rose petal lips.

"Are you seriously doubting my feelings for you?" he growled out, turning to fully face her.

She chewed on her bottom lip and shrugged.

"Seriously? You feel me just as much as I feel you. Has anything ever made you feel anything that would indicate I don't want you for the rest of my damn life? I don't care if there are monsters hiding under your bed every night. I'll fight for you and with you and keep you safe. Never fucking doubt that or me again."

He pushed to his feet and stomped out of the room. He had to Shift. He had to run for a few minutes to expel some of the angry energy and anxiety over the newest bull shit. But he wouldn't leave Hollyn alone.

As he stepped to the front door and looked onto his front porch, he realized he wouldn't be leaving her alone. Luke was sitting on the top step, just like he was every single morning.

Luke glanced back at Noah as he opened the door. "Need to run," he ground out as his bones began to pop and Shift.

"Go," Luke said, turning back to stare at the woods some more. "I've got her."

Bear exploded from Noah before he was passed the trucks. His big paws slammed onto the gravel and then took off like a bullet, putting distance between him and Hollyn. Even this far away, he could feel her regret, her sorrow, and that fucking fear that gutted him. He hated it. He wished he could take it away, make it disappear. He wished *they* could disappear.

But she was right. No matter how far they went, no matter how much time passed, no matter where they lived or what was going on in their lives, there would always be someone who'd see her as a trinket, a prize, something to get rich from instead of seeing the beautiful, funny, strong, vibrant woman.

Twigs and leaves crunched and cracked under his paws, animals scurried away and hid in the brush. They didn't need to worry; Bear wasn't hunting. He was thinking, trying to come up with some way to keep his mate safe.

Short of wrapping her in bubble wrap and locking her in a padded room, there was no way to keep her out of harm's way.

Maybe the best thing to do was draw all the fuckers out, get them all in one place, and eliminate each threat head on. But how? He refused to use Hollyn as bait, but someone already found her. And he had no idea whether she was a threat or not.

Another Fae, a female Fairy in the area, and she'd found Hollyn. Could she be helpful to Hollyn? Or would it just raise the stakes having two in such close proximity? Maybe she could help keep Hollyn safe and they'd all keep both women safe.

Too much. Too much shit at one time. At least when they'd fought Deathport, Tammen, and Horine Pride, they knew what to expect. It was one threat, one group with a stick up their asses. Now?

Too much.

Sorrow and shock hit Noah in the heart, making him stumble. His bear lifted his snout in the air and inhaled deep. A new scent. Not Clan. Not Pack.

Bear made a wide turn and ran full force back to the territory, back to Hollyn, back to his mate. Someone made her sad. Someone hurt her.

Mine, Bear growled in Noah's head.

Feet pounding the ground, Bear pushed harder to get to their mate, to get to Hollyn. *Hurry*, Noah urged in Bear's head.

Voices carried to him on the wind, male voices, female voices. Carter, Luke, Colton, Shawnee, Hollyn…and who? Who was that last voice? Was she a threat? Noah didn't feel fear coming from Hollyn, still the sorrow, still the shock.

The second Noah burst through the trees, Luke Shifted and ran toward him, cutting him off before he got too close.

"She's safe, brother," Carter called over the distance. Colton stood close, his eyes bright, never leaving the woman standing in front of Hollyn. It was the dark-haired woman from last night. This was the Fairy. She'd tracked Hollyn to Moe's, then found her at home.

He'd been running. Noah had been running through the woods when she'd showed up. What if it'd been someone else? What if he hadn't gotten back to her in time? He was an idiot. Selfish. He'd put his own needs ahead of Hollyn's safety.

Bear paced back and forth along the tree line, his eyes on Hollyn, on the woman, while Noah begged for his skin back.

Need to talk to her. Need to find out what's going on. The longer he went without permanently marking Hollyn, the further out of control his bear was spiraling.

Luke's bear growled a warning, but he didn't move, didn't get out of Noah's path. He wouldn't let him do something he couldn't take back. Noah begged his bear, his eyes going to Hollyn. He could feel her calling to him, beckoning him forward without saying a word.

She needs me. She needs us, Noah told his bear.

With a huff of frustration, Bear released his hold and let Noah take his skin back. But he made it as slow as possible, forcing Noah to suffer every fucking step.

Chapter Eleven

Hollyn stared at Noah in panic as his bear paced the tree line, his bright gaze going back and forth between Hollyn and Melinda. She needed him to stop, needed Noah the man, not his bear. Needed him to understand.

"Mate," Hollyn called out. Melinda's head whipped around, her eyes wide in surprise. Last thing she expected to hear, apparently. "It's okay," she said, forcing a smile and trying to block her emotion from Noah while trying to calm his animal.

Slowly, Bear gave Noah his skin back. By the time it was over, Noah knelt on the ground, his fists against the packed dirt, panting through the pain as a sheen of sweat broke out along his body.

Hollyn took a step away from Melinda and toward her mate. He pushed to his feet, his hand immediately moving to cup his junk and hide himself from the newcomer. Turning on her heel, Hollyn ran up the stairs and into the house and grabbed Noah a t-shirt and a pair of sweats. She carried them out to Noah and handed them over, using her own body as a shield while he dressed.

And then she took him by the hand and guided him over to the only Fairy she'd ever met beside her parents. "Noah, this is Melinda. This is who I've been feeling all this time."

Luke padded over to them, still in his bear form. He slowly positioned himself until he was standing between Hollyn and Melinda. She might not have noticed it, but Hollyn knew Luke didn't like the stranger close to Hollyn, to his Clan sister.

"She's a Fairy, like me," Hollyn said, unable to hold back the excited smile.

Noah's eyes were narrowed on Melinda. He didn't trust her. Hollyn could feel it, feel his fear of this woman. He still stuck his hand out to Melinda, wrapping it around hers when she slowly slipped her hand into his.

"You called him mate," Melinda said when she pulled her hand back. "He's a Shifter." She didn't pull her eyes from Noah as she spoke, and something like disgust flashed through her dark as night eyes. Hers did the same as Hollyn's, changing with her emotions.

That didn't sit well with Hollyn. She didn't know this woman enough to care about her opinion, but Melinda was looking at Hollyn's mate as if she wished he'd disappear. There was no fear in her eyes. Why the hell wasn't Melinda scared of Noah, or any of Blackwater for that matter. They were Shifters. She was a Fairy. She should've been terrified. Yet, she'd wandered right onto the territory and straight to Noah's door. She didn't even react when all three men and Shawnee stepped onto their porch to see what was going on.

"Because he's my mate," Hollyn said, turning a frown on Melinda. She was excited to meet someone of her kind, but she'd be damned if she let a complete stranger disrespect the love of her life.

Hollyn moved closer to Noah and took his hand again, threading her fingers through his and stepping into his side.

Melinda's eyes dropped to where Noah and Hollyn were linked then back to Hollyn's face. "I just hoped…" But she trailed off and didn't finish her thought.

"You hoped what?" Hollyn asked.

Hollyn could feel Noah's anxiety because of their link. But she could feel it rolling from the rest of the Clan, as well. They were wary of this woman, wary of her sudden appearance.

"I'd hoped you'd join me in tracking down more of our kind. There's safety in numbers," she said, but something about her words felt wrong, strained…like a lie.

"How did you find Hollyn?" Carter asked, his tree trunk arms crossed over his chest. He'd stayed calm and collected since Melinda showed up, but Hollyn didn't miss the tick in his jaw. Or the way Colton seemed tense and strung tight. And Luke, well Luke was as intense as ever, his eyes bright from the second he stepped onto his porch.

Melinda tensed slightly, just barely, but Hollyn caught it. "I, uh…I knew her parents."

Lie. Total lie. In the thirteen years Hollyn had with her parents, she'd never met another Fae. They didn't have Fae friends coming and going, no family, just them.

"Try again," Noah said as if reading Hollyn's mind.

"I did. When Hollyn was a baby. You just don't remember me," Melinda said to Hollyn.

"That still doesn't explain how you found her," Carter said, taking a slow step closer.

Melinda dropped her head and sighed dramatically. "I've been following you for years, Hollyn. I've kept an eye on you, tried to protect you."

"Didn't do too good of a job," Colton mumbled under his breath.

"I was too late. I know that. I was…I was out trying to find more of our kind. When I got back, Hollyn was gone. The traffickers had gotten her and I didn't know where she was."

Tears glistened in Melinda's eyes. She looked regretful. "I'm sorry. I should've been there to protect you."

As a tear rolled down Melinda's cheek, Hollyn released her hold on Noah and moved toward Melinda. "It wasn't your fault. You had to stay hidden, too," Hollyn said, laying a hand on Melinda's shoulder. She trembled once with a held back sob. Well, shit. She hadn't meant to hurt her feelings.

Melinda raised a hand and dashed away the tear. "I'm just so sorry, Hollyn." She reached forward and waited for Hollyn to step in for a hug. She'd never been much of a hugger, but Melinda seemed to need one.

Hollyn let Melinda wrap her arms around her back and she patted Melinda's back lightly. Her eyes met Shawnee who did not look convinced by Melinda's show of emotion. She locked eyes with Hollyn and shook her head, just a quick side to side.

When Melinda loosened her hold, Noah pulled Hollyn back to his side, wrapping an arm around her shoulders protectively and possessively. "She's safe with me," Noah said. "You don't need to protect her anymore."

Was he politely telling Melinda to hit the road?

"But we need to find others of our kind," Melinda said, reaching for Hollyn again.

Hollyn frowned at Melinda and shook her head. "I'm not going anywhere. This is my family."

“They’re not your family. They’re predators. Shifters. Why do you think they want you here?”

“Because they love me,” Hollyn said, jutting her chin out. “My magic chose Noah. We’re bound.”

“He hasn’t bitten you, has he?” she asked, her eyes wide and full of panic.

“Or course not,” Hollyn said.

“Then you’re not really his mate.”

“She’s my mate,” Noah said, his words laced with a growl as his arm tightened around her shoulder.

That look of disgust and disapproval was back and Hollyn had just about enough. “I’m glad you found me and I appreciate you watching out for me after my parents died, but I’m grown. I have a husband now, a family of my own. I’m not going with you, but I wish you the best.”

“Husband,” Melinda spat. “You didn’t marry him. And he hasn’t bitten you. He can’t. You both know that, don’t you?”

Any question she’d had about the risk of a Shifter’s bite was answered in that one statement from this woman. Hollyn felt defeated for a brief second. Part of her wanted to carry Noah’s scar, wanted that change in her blood, wanted any Shifter she encountered to know she belonged to an incredible man.

“I think it’s time to go,” Carter said, ever the diplomat.

Melinda turned only her eyes to Carter before looking back to Hollyn. “I’m glad to see you’re safe,” she said, then gave Hollyn her back as she made her way to her car.

It purred to life easily. It was one of those expensive Mercedes with shiny wheels and an almost silent engine. Melinda looked back at Hollyn, her brows raised in question. She was giving Hollyn a chance to change her mind. She didn’t need to bother. Lifting her chin, she stared Melinda down until she turned back in her seat and pulled out slowly, the dings of gravel hitting the bottom of the fifty thousand dollar car surprisingly satisfying.

“That was interesting,” Hollyn said, turning back to the Clan once Melinda’s car disappeared around the bend.

"How the fuck did she find you? She never answered that question," Noah said. "She said she'd been following you but lost you after the traffickers took you. So how did she know you were here? How did she know to look for you at Moe's?"

"Can she follow your magic?" Carter asked.

"Possibly? I mean, I've felt her in the area for a few days now." The thought of being able to locate others of her kind through her magic was intriguing.

"I don't like this," Colton said. "It's just a little convenient. If she's been looking after you all these years, why introduce herself now?"

"Kind of what I was thinking," Shawnee said.

Luke Shifted back, but didn't bother hiding his nudity. "She's fucking trouble," he said as he walked across the gravel with such ease, like the gravel wasn't biting into his bare feet.

Hollyn and Shawnee both averted their eyes as he passed, but she'd caught an eyeful. Apparently, all bears were hung. Two growls came from Noah and Colton.

"What?" Hollyn asked as innocently as possible. Wasn't her fault her Clan was full of good looking guys, or that Shifters had no problem with nudity.

"I'm back to saying it's not a good idea for you to be at the bar," Noah said.

"And I still say it's the safest place for me. Hell, even old John took up for me. I don't think anyone would just stand by while some asshole drags me away kicking and screaming. And Melinda isn't a threat. I didn't detect fire magic on her, so there's no way she could win if she turned out to be some nut job or something."

"She's right, Noah," Shawnee said. "If you leave her here, we'll all be at work." Shawnee raised her hand the second Noah opened his mouth. "And I'm not staying behind. Even if I did, the two of us against we don't know how many? You like those odds?"

"No," Colton answered for Noah.

"And no way am I hanging out in Big River when the babies are there."

"She's fucking trouble!" Luke yelled from his cabin. It was muffled, but Hollyn heard it.

Something about Melinda did rub Hollyn the wrong way, but she couldn't put her finger on it. Maybe it was just the shock of meeting another Fairy. Or the feeling of another's magic on her skin. Whatever it was, Hollyn didn't like the thought of being alone.

Noah dragged a rough hand down his face, smoothing his beard before dropping his hand by his side. "Fuck." She hated that she'd caused him so much trouble since she'd stepped onto his porch. But to her defense, she'd never asked to be there. She had no desire to leave now, but originally, the thought of being shacked with a group of Shifters she didn't know from Adam seemed like a nightmare.

It had become a dream. Hollyn couldn't ask for more than the love she got from these people. Even Luke's outburst from inside his house gave her the feels. Dude didn't talk much, but he cared about her, cared about her safety.

"She's right, Noah. She's safer at Moe's. One of us is usually there at some point. You'll be by her side all damn day. And all you got to do is call one of us if there's more than you and Shawnee can handle," Carter said.

Colton growled deep and low at the mention of his mate fighting without him there to watch her back.

Noah's anger and worry was causing Hollyn's heart rate to race, just like Noah's. She followed the thread of magic and focused on Bear's energy, focused on his calmness. Now that Melinda was gone, Bear had gone back to observing, watching over Hollyn, watching over his mate.

"I can feel that," Noah said, surprising Hollyn enough she started.

"Feel what?"

"Whatever your doing to my animal."

"Can you pull from his energy?" she asked.

"What do you mean?"

"Can you feel his calmness? He's fine now that Melinda's gone. I was trying to focus on him because you're about to give me a heart attack," she said and smiled to soften the words.

Noah pressed the heel of his hand to his chest and rubbed, like he was trying to feel his bear. Slowly, he shook his head. They were different entities living inside one body. She'd have thought they'd feel each other's emotions, not just hear each other's thoughts.

Hollyn stepped closer and wrapped her arms around his waist, tipping her head back to look into his eyes. "Then feel mine," she said softly, meaning it for his ears but knew the Clan could hear her.

Under her hands, Noah's body began to relax and his heart slowed. A small smile tipped up his lips. "You're amazing," he said as softly as she'd spoken. He lowered and sipped at her lips, just a sweet kiss full of affection.

****

Noah kept stealing glances at Hollyn as he drove them to Moe's. Every day she did something else that surprised him, and he'd truly believed nothing could surprise him anymore. He'd seen the worst of people, the best of people, and everything in between. Yet, there she was, connected as fully to his animal as she was to him. Only she could calm his beast, only she could calm Noah.

"I love you," Noah said. "You know that, right?"

Hollyn smiled over at him. "Of course I do."

Every day. Shit. Every minute, his heart grew for this woman. And so did his fear. Something about Melinda wasn't sitting right with him. He should've been excited for Hollyn, excited that she'd found someone of her kind, but Melinda looked at Noah and his Clan like demons. Or bugs under her shoe. And she'd wanted to take Hollyn away.

But there was more. He just…he couldn't figure it out. Why did it feel like this woman was the key to ending all this bull shit for Hollyn? Maybe she was telling the truth and had been looking after Hollyn all those years. But she hadn't been able to keep her out of the hands of the traffickers. Some protection she was.

His mushy feelings quickly turned to anger as Noah ran through the entire conversation, and the fact she'd never answered how the hell she'd found Hollyn. Even if she had been following Hollyn all these years, she'd said herself she'd lost her after the traffickers took her. Hollyn had no idea if Melinda had been able to follow her magic as some kind of beacon.

Too many fucking questions and what ifs and not enough answers.

Noah pulled his truck onto the gravel parking lot and killed the engine. He stared at the front door, leaning his head against the rest.

"Talk to me," Hollyn said, turning in her seat and resting her cheek on the passenger side rest. "I can feel you freaking out. Just get it out of your system."

Noah rolled his head to look at her. "Get it out of my system? You think talking it out will make it go away?" he asked. He didn't mean to sound so asshole-ish, but he couldn't control the anger in his tone.

She raised one brow and pressed her lips into a thin line and Noah felt a wave of heat hit him square in the fucking chest the same time her eyes flashed to that dark midnight color. He winced and raised both brows at her. "Did you just try to fry me?"

"Did you just become an asshole to me?" she threw back at him.

Hollyn shoved from her seat and stomped up to the bar's door. She didn't turn to see if he followed, just waited with her arms crossed under her boobs. Okay. That was fucking cute. He knew if he told her he kind of liked when she got pissed, it would just piss her off even more. But yeah. She was even hotter when she was all riled up.

Inhaling through his nose and blowing it out through his mouth, Noah tried to calm his heart rate. He tried to focus on how seeing Hollyn all huffy made him feel. He focused on how cute she'd looked on the drive when she nodded her head along to the music and danced in her seat as if she couldn't care less if anyone passing by saw her.

She turned and looked at him over her shoulder. Her black irises bled to sapphire and she had a faint smile on her lips. The heat was gone, both from his chest and her eyes.

"Is that something you can do to anyone?" Noah asked as he unlocked the bar door.

"Nope. Just you. Aren't you lucky?!" she said. There was still a crap ton of attitude, but Noah could feel her softening toward him through their connection. The longer he was bound to Hollyn, the more he was growing to love that shit. There'd be none of that *fine* shit if he asked her if something was wrong. He'd just feel it, whether it was hurt or anger or whatever.

Noah watched her ass sway as she moved toward the bar. When she looked back and caught him, he shrugged. "What? Couldn't help myself," he said.

That broke the last of the ice. Her smile widened as she shook her head. "And they call Nova the perv."

"Hey, I just checked out my mate's ass. I didn't write about it."

Noah worked side by side with Hollyn, getting everything ready, stocking the cooler, prepping the kitchen. Just before he unlocked the front door for the public, he caught Hollyn chewing on her bottom lip, a far away look in her eyes.

"What's up?" he asked. He didn't feel much coming from her, just the usual she'd been feeling from day one.

"Do you ever regret it?" she asked after a few moments of her staring at him.

"Regret what?"

"Mating with a Fairy? Not being able to mark me? Mating with someone with so much freaking baggage."

"For one thing, it's not your fucking baggage. No woman should have to worry about that shit," Noah said, turning and moving closer to the bar. He leaned over the top and reached for her hand, threading his fingers through hers and pressing his palm to hers. "And why the hell would I regret mating with a Fairy? Why should it matter?"

"Because you can't mark me." She sucked that bottom lip between her teeth and Noah reached up to pull it free, rubbing the pad of his thumb across it.

"I get to mark you constantly instead of once."

Her lips slowly pulled into a smile. "Perv," she said, attempting to pull her hand away.

He tightened his grip and pulled her closer to the bar, leaning forward to press a kiss to her lips.

"Never for one fucking second think I could ever regret being with you," he said before kissing her once more.

It was time to get the day started. Old John would be there soon and he'd throw a fit if the door was locked. He'd do his usual and prop himself on the bar, drinking the day away, only ordering an appetizer when he was close to falling off the barstool.

Hollyn nodded when he glanced back at her. It was time for yet another fucking day at the bar. Another day where he spent every waking hour serving drinks to Shifters. But as he winked at Hollyn when he passed to round the bar, he realized how much it no longer sucked. As long as Hollyn was working beside him, he didn't mind being there so much.

Chapter Twelve

Hollyn lie in the crook of Noah's shoulder, playing with his fingers on the arm wrapped around her. She'd mentioned a few times about not having a family, but she'd yet to tell him why. It was time. It was time for him to know why she'd wanted to run away when Aron told them he couldn't locate the traffickers. She needed him to know why she needed to protect them so badly.

"You still awake?" she whispered into the dark.

"Mmhmm," he said sleepily.

Maybe now wasn't the time. They'd gotten home a little late and spent the last hour touching and tasting each other.

"What's wrong?" he asked when she was still mulling over in her head whether she should bring up something so heavy before bed time.

"Nothing," she lied and turned to lay her cheek on his chest.

"You realize I can tell when you're lying," he said, kissing the top of her head.

She smiled against his chest and sighed. "It can wait until tomorrow," she said, keeping her voice quiet to preserve the peace of the dark, comfy bedroom.

Noah moved beneath her, then the room was lit up by the lamp on his nightstand. Hollyn squinted against the brightness after lying in the dark for so long.

Positioning Hollyn so that she was on her side, Noah turned on his pillow to face her. "Tell me," he said.

His hair was in need of a cut and sticking up everywhere. His beard was messy from their make out session before they'd made love. But his eyes, his eyes held so much love and warmth she just wanted to swim in their depths.

Hollyn reached forward and softly touched his beard. It looked like it would be coarse and scratchy, but he took such good care of it that it was almost as soft as his hair. For some reason, petting him as if she were petting him and his bear, calmed her racing heart.

“I told you that I haven’t had a family in a long time,” she said, raising her eyes to meet his. He nodded, but didn’t say anything. “I haven’t had anyone since my thirteenth birthday.”

Sadness hit her hard as she allowed her mind to go back to that time, to that day, to the last time she’d see her parents alive again.

“My parents were like I am now, always moving, always hiding. You know how rare it is for two Fae to be together, but they’d found each other. And then I came alone. As you can imagine, the fact I was born from two full-blood Fae terrified my parents. I didn’t just have Fae blood, I was an Elemental Fairy with a gift of fire.” A tiny smile pulled at her lips. “They figured out my gift when I burned my mom’s nipple when she was breast feeding me.”

Noah grimaced and huffed a sound.

“Normally, our gifts, no matter how big or small, don’t manifest until around puberty. Usually around ten for girls and thirteen for boys. They knew I could make fire as an infant. I could call my magic by the time I was eight. It freaked my parents out.”

“They were scared someone would find out,” Noah said, figuring it out before she said much else.

“Exactly. The Fae are already worth a lot of money. But imagine if anyone had found out that I was not only pure blood, but had a strong gift. Not only would I be worth a lot to traffickers, but to any human government who might discover my existence. I’m sure someone like me would be a lot easier to explain than someone like you.” She smiled but it didn’t reach her eyes.

“So they kept you hidden,” Noah said, reaching out to play with her hair that had fallen over her shoulder.

“We weren’t in one place for longer than a few months at a time. My mom homeschooled me, taught me how to read and write and all that. There was no way they’d put me in regular school with a bunch of human kids. Could you imagine if some kid made me mad and I shot fire at him?”

That time, the smile on Noah’s face was genuine.

“We moved the day before my thirteenth birthday. This time, my parents decided to try to hide among humans instead of living in the middle of nowhere. They figured with so many eyes everywhere, no way would anyone try anything." She felt the tears burning the backs of her eyes as that day played in the back of her mind. "My mon always felt bad that I couldn't really make any friends, so she decided to throw me a birthday party with just the three of us. She went out and got some junk food, a cake, ice cream, even some balloons. I was in my room reading and she called me out. It was the coolest thing I'd ever seen. There were pink and purple balloons everywhere, hanging on the wall, all over the floor so they'd float when I'd kick them."

Her chest was growing tight. The closer she got to the part of their death, the harder it was to breathe.

"Someone must've seen my mom and known what she was when she went shopping. That night, after we'd eaten until we could barely move and squished onto the crappy love seat that came with the fully furnished apartment to watch a movie, someone knocked on the door."

Noah took her hand and held it tight, staying silent and letting her get through the worst day of her life.

Her mom's eyes widened as she looked at her dad. Slowly, her dad stood, holding a finger to his lips. They didn't know a single person in that town. There was no reason for anyone to be knocking on their door. Even if it was a neighbor wanting to welcome them into the building, her dad wouldn't answer the door.

Reaching down, her dad turned the knob to silence the movie. Hollyn remembered thinking that was useless. Whoever was at the door would've already heard the sounds coming through the door.

Her mom was hugging Hollyn tightly to her side, her eyes full of terror. And all Hollyn could do was whimper. She'd never seen either of her parents so afraid in her life. Her dad held up his hand and motioned for the two of them to head to the back of the apartment and lock themselves in one of the bedrooms.

Hollyn's mom hurried Hollyn down the hallway and quickly closed the door silently behind them, turning the lock in place and holding her ear to the door.

"Who is it, mom?" Hollyn whispered.

Her mom held up a hand for Hollyn to be quiet. Mom slowly stepped from the door, her eyes wide. And then she turned those eyes on Hollyn. She'd never seen her mom like this, had never seen her eyes so empty, so cold, do dark.

"Run," she said a second before Hollyn heard her dad yell and a thump echo from the living room.

Hollyn whimpered and backed away from the door. Run? Where was she supposed to go? It was a two bedroom apartment on the third floor.

She couldn't leave her parents there alone. Raising her hand, she called a ball of flame forth and moved to throw it at the door the second it opened.

"No!" her mom said, hurrying to her side and curling Hollyn's hand closed over the flame. "Never show anyone what you can do. Ever. Understand? It'll be even worse. Just run. Please. I love you so much. Please."

Her mom pushed her toward the window, shoved it open, then helped Hollyn climb through the window. "I love you," she whispered before sliding it shut as quietly as possible.

Hollyn hesitated a second on the fire escape. Where was she supposed to go? What was she supposed to do?

A sound she'd never forget echoed through the room and froze Hollyn's steps. Her mother screamed a second before an animal snarled and howled. Shifters. Shifter had found them. Did that mean they'd take her mother and sell her? Would they try to force her to have babies with them?

Her mother began to say something, to beg, but her words were cut off and an odd gurgling sound took their place. And then there was another thud, like the one she'd heard from the living room.

As if she could see through the walls, she knew her parents were dead. Could feel it. Could feel that magical thread between them fade to nothing.

Slowly at first, Hollyn backed down the stairs on shaky legs. Another howl pierced the night and had her legs moving faster. She descended the stairs as fast as she could without tumbling down headfirst.

When her feet hit pavement, she ran into the night, never looking back, never checking to see if anyone was following her. She ran until the cool air burned her lungs, until her legs felt like they'd been frozen in ice. When she could run anymore, she found a drainpipe and climbed into it, bringing her knees to her chest and turning herself into a tiny ball in hopes no one could see her.

She'd been hiding ever since. Until the assholes had found her. Until Aron had saved her. Until she'd met and fell for Noah. Until she'd bound them for life.

"I'm so sorry," Noah whispered, bringing her hand to his mouth to feather her knuckles with kisses. He reached both arms out and Hollyn happily wiggled into them, pressing her cheek against his chest as tears flowed down her cheeks and into her hair.

He held her close, his big, warm hands stroking up and down her spine as he kissed her temple. And then he pulled back enough to look into her face. "You showed me your fire the first day we met," he said with furrowed brows.

"I guess my magic already knew I could trust you," she said, shrugging up the shoulder that wasn't wedged against the mattress.

Hollyn felt the moment Noah's heart swelled with so much love. She'd had people in her life who loved her, and now they were gone. Then, she'd had a new family take her in and love her. She would stop at nothing to protect them. Even if it meant revealing her gift to the world.

****

Sunday rolled around again, and Hollyn hadn't felt Melinda's presence again. Opening her eyes, she sighed at the weight across her middle. Noah had rolled onto his side and thrown an arm across her waist, claiming her and protecting her even in his sleep.

She hated to leave the warmth of his body, but she needed a shower before work. Last night had been one of the busiest nights Moe's had ever had, according to Noah. They'd both had to tend the bar while Shawnee ran around like a chicken with her head caught off to deliver so many drinks. Most of the people were there to see Hollyn perform, but they didn't care who made their drinks, as long as they could still watch Hollyn.

Exhaustion had wracked her body the whole way home and they'd both shuffled toward the bedroom, stripped to nothing but underwear, then collapsed into the bed. They hadn't even made love last night, which was odd for them. The only time they'd gone to sleep without fooling around was the night Hollyn had gotten so drunk she'd passed out.

As Hollyn tried to wiggle out from under Noah's arm, his hold tightened and he pulled her closer.

"Where you going? It's not time to get up yet," he said, his voice hoarse with sleep.

"I need a shower," she said, then giggled when he buried his face in the crook of her neck and nipped at her.

Her giggles quickly turned into a moan as his lips found the sensitive spot below her ear the same time his hand smoothed down her body and slipped beneath her panties. He had her panting and begging for him within minutes.

"Nope," he said when she tried to drag him onto of her. Instead, he slid down the bed, taking her panties with him, and made love to her with his mouth. As she cried out with her release, he quickly moved up and thrust into her, holding still to feel the way her muscles clamped around him. "That's so fucking sexy," he said, lowering his face and licking the spot where his bear wanted to mark her.

Within seconds, Noah was pounding fast and hard into her, hooking one of her legs over his arm to open her further. And then he pulled out, flipped her onto her stomach, and pulled her ass up, pressing a hand against her shoulders to keep her upper half against the mattress.

He was slow when he entered her this time, feeding her an inch at a time until Hollyn was squirming and pushing back on him to get him to move.

"You want it?" he growled out and Hollyn wondered if Bear was there, too.

"Yes. I want it so bad," she begged, pushing back again.

He chuckled that deep, sexy sound she loved so much, reared back, and then slammed his cock into her. Hollyn cried out as stars exploded behind her lids. Somehow, he was prolonging her first orgasm. Did that make it multiples? She'd never experienced that, but she couldn't imagine it would feel any better than what Noah was doing to her right now.

With his hands on her hips, Noah took her hard and fast, his grunts mixing with her panting and moaning. It was erotic. It was primal. It was sexy as hell.

Bending over her back, Noah licked along her spine, then reached around her and used his fingers on her clit.

"I want to hear you come one more time," he said, his mouth so close to her ear his warm breath tickled.

Just hearing him say the words made her tighten everywhere until she imploded and exploded from the inside out. She heard Noah's name on her lips over and over, but barely recognized her own voice.

Noah pulled out, placed his shaft along the crack of her ass, and spilled on her back. They'd gotten carried away and forgotten the condom again. And once again, Noah had enough foresight to keep from finishing inside of her and risking pregnancy.

With each hot jet hitting her flesh, Noah grunted, the sound so deep and guttural, making Hollyn's sex pulse with need all over again.

She once again wondered if they'd ever get tired of touching each other, feeling each other, hearing each other come. As far as she was concerned, she'd never tire of feeling Noah inside of her or his rough hands on her body.

Noah stood and grabbed one of his t-shirts from the ground, using it to clean Hollyn's back. "We've got to stop risking that," Noah grumbled as he tossed the soiled shirt across the room and into the hamper.

He helped her to her knees then to her feet. "I want to close the bar today," he said, his eyes roaming her face before lowering, a flash of bright amber lighting his irises from behind.

"What? Why?"

He'd told her he could count how many times he'd either closed early or just closed altogether on one hand and it always involved someone else's needs.

"I want to spend the day with you. I want to do what Shawnee and Colton do and hang out on the couch and watch TV all day."

Could he, though? Could he do nothing all day without the anxiety of not being at work ruining it for him.

"And I want to make love to you as many times as I want without feeling rushed."

And she suddenly didn't care if he could take the day off without being anxious.

Hollyn let Noah lead her to the shower. "So you're saying you want to spend the day vegging on the couch and worshipping my body?" she teased as he turned on the spray.

"Yep." That was all he said as he turned to check her out. Every time he looked at her it was like he was seeing her for the first time. Every single time she was naked in front of him, Noah got an instant boner and Hollyn could feel his want and need for her. She got it. She really did. Because everything about Noah turned her on.

Noah held his hand out to her and helped her step into the shower. He got in behind her and used his bare hands to wash her, soaping them up with her body wash and slowly and gently running them across every inch of her body. Within minutes, she was panting with need.

"You did that on purpose," she said and was fully aware of how breathy she sounded.

"This is just a little foreplay," he said, standing and guiding her into the spray to rinse off the suds.

He was hard and ready for her, but didn't take her against the shower wall, didn't bend her over the sink, didn't even try to take her on the bed when he carried her to the bedroom to get dressed.

"Isn't getting dressed a huge waste of time? I mean, you did say you wanted to worship my body all day."

"Technically, I said I wanted to hang out and make love." His eyes held a slight glow as he sat on the edge of the bed and watched her dress. He'd already pulled on a pair of sweats that he hadn't destroyed Shifting and a tank top that hugged his muscles in the most tantalizing way and made her mouth water.

If he didn't want her to constantly want to jump his bones why the hell had he dressed like a sex pot?

Noah smiled as Hollyn pouted. "Don't worry. I plan on making you scream a few more times today," he said in that gravelly voice of his.

He kissed her on the tip of her nose as he stood. "I'm going to make my mate breakfast. Then we're going to sprawl out on the couch and eat and watch movies all day."

He turned the corner, leaving Hollyn alone in the room. His couch wasn't exactly big enough for them to sprawl out on together, but she didn't mind. As hot as she was for him after his attentions in the shower, she was excited about spending the day with him, getting to know him more, talking to him about something other than work, Fairies, and psycho Shifters.

Hollyn's grin was wide as she jogged from the bedroom. She wanted to witness Noah actually using his kitchen for something more than just making coffee or sandwiches. In the month she'd been in Blackwater territory, she'd yet to see him cook anything at home. He cook at the bar all the time, but that was bar food, burgers and fries and other greasy food. He was intent on being domestic and feeding his mate.

He moved around the space with ease, pulling eggs and bacon from the fridge. When had he gone shopping? Or were those in there for a while? Surely, he wouldn't feed her old stuff.

"I had Shawnee go shopping for me when she got off last night," Noah said when he turned and caught her expression.

"She got off late," Hollyn said.

"Yeah, but *Wal-mart* is a twenty-four hour place." He winked and turned back to the sizzling bacon.

Hollyn took a seat at the table, propped her elbows on top, and rested her chin in her hands. There was something so homey about the sound and smell of bacon cooking. There was something homey about Noah making that bacon for her.

And then it hit her; this wasn't Noah's house. This was her home. He hadn't exactly asked her to move in, but he'd been adamant about her not leaving. After twenty years, she had a real home, not a temporary place until she had to run for the next town. She had a family, a husband. All that was missing was the white picket fence and dog.

And kids.

She'd never thought about motherhood, feared it, wondered about her ability to nurture another little person. But with Noah, she wanted to try. She wanted to see a child who was a mixture of the two of them. Would their child be a bear like his daddy or a Fairy like her momma? Would he have brown eyes like Noah or blue eyes like Hollyn?

And could they really keep their child safe from the hunters and traffickers?

She hadn't realized she'd zoned out until Noah bent into her line of sight, his brows pulled together.

"What's wrong?" he asked.

She shook her head, worried if she tried to speak, emotion would clog her throat and make her croak out the words.

"I felt a wave of sadness," he said, rounding the table and kneeling in front of her.

"You're going to burn the bacon," she said with a sniffle.

"Then I'll get more."

She dropped her eyes to where his hands rested on her knees. "I was just thinking about kids. And how pretty our kids would be. And how we can't guarantee their safety. I could never put my own child through what I went through. Hiding and scrounging for my next meal until I was old enough to work." A single tear rolled over her lashes and left a hot trail down her cheek.

Noah wiped it away and tipped her face up with a finger under her chin. "If we ever decide we want kids, we will keep them safe. But I'm just as content to have you in my life for as long as I'm alive."

"You'd be happy with no kids?" she asked. It made her sad to think they couldn't risk having children because of the rest of the world. It was like their choice was taken away from them.

"Big River has kids. And someday, I'm sure Colton and Shawnee will have kids. We'll just be the kind of aunt and uncle who spoil the shit out of them."

He pushed to his feet, kissed the top of Hollyn's head, then returned to the stove. "Still not burned. Damn, I'm good."

That made her laugh. And she knew he'd said it for that reason, to cheer her up and get her mind off the heavy crap.

Once the bacon was done, he whipped up a bunch of eggs and poured it directly into the hot bacon grease.

"You're going to make me fat," she said, standing and stepping behind him, wrapping her arms around his waist.

"And I'd still think you were the hottest woman I've ever seen and would continue to want you as bad as I do now," he said without missing a beat.

He knew all the right things to say, always knew how to make her blush, knew how to rev her up and how to calm her down. They might not have been together as long as their friends were with their mates, but they knew each other. Maybe not the simple things like favorite colors or movies, but the things that counted, the things that were in their hearts.

"I love you," Hollyn said.

Noah glanced over his shoulder, a sweet smile showing his pretty white teeth. "I know. I can feel it."

She sighed a girly sound and released her hold on him, moving back to the table while Noah plated the food and carried it over, setting a plate in front of her and one in front of the seat directly across from her.

They ate in comfortable silence, occasionally glancing up at each other. But she knew he could feel her happiness at the simple gesture. Hollyn finished first, pushing her plate away and leaning back in her seat. "I'm stuffed," she said, then giggled when Noah shoved enough food in his mouth to make his cheeks puff out. "Dork."

Hollyn sucked her lips into her mouth to hide the smile when Noah cocked a brow at her. They played at the bar and were sometimes silly in the bedroom. But this was the first time they had nowhere to go, nothing pressing to do. They could be themselves, cut up, tease each other and do whatever the hell they wanted for the rest of the day.

She couldn't help but wonder after getting to spend a whole day alone with Noah if she'd be able to go back to work. Who was she kidding? She was just as much a workaholic as Noah. She loved that he'd intentionally shut the bar down so neither of them had to work. But they'd both be back behind that bar tomorrow morning.

But not today. Today, her man was all hers.

Chapter Thirteen

Noah thought he'd planned their day alone well. He'd known Saturday night, watching Hollyn busting her ass for fourteen hours straight that she needed a day off. And as much as he didn't like her out in the open the way she was when she worked at Moe's, he really didn't like the thought of her home alone. Even if Shawnee stayed behind, it would be just the two of them. And since Aron had no idea how many of those fuckers were out there, none of them wanted to take the chance.

After he'd sent Shawnee home for the night, he'd given her a bunch of money and tipped her an extra hundred to run out and grab him some food for meals and a bunch of junk so they wouldn't have to leave the couch unless they wanted to. She'd bought just about anything Noah would have. The problem with his plan to veg all day was that he didn't have cable, and only had a couple of old ass, out of date DVDs.

He tried to be smooth and hid in the bathroom while he typed out a text to Shawnee, begging her to borrow a few movies. He knew she and Colton liked to snuggle on the couch and watch different crap when she was off work.

Shawnee sent back a thumbs up. Noah flushed the unused toilet and ran the faucet so it looked like he'd used the bathroom. By the time he stepped out, he heard light foot steps on his front porch. Hollyn pulled the door open before she even knocked.

"I'm sorry. I totally forgot to leave these last night when I brought the food over," Shawnee said, waiting until Hollyn glanced down at the stack of Blu Ray discs in her hand before winking at Noah.

One problem with her story – Noah had an older DVD player, not a Blu Ray. Shit. "Are any of those regular DVDs?" Noah asked, looking over Hollyn's shoulder to see what movies Shawnee had brought them.

Shawnee frowned and flipped through them. "Um…these two are," she said, her brows pulled together and up as she gave him an *uh oh* face.

“Those are fine. I love both of those movies,” Hollyn said, taking the only two DVDs probably in existence other than his weak collection.

Noah checked out the titles: *Friday the 13th* and Stephen King’s *It*, the original version. His girl was a horror fan? Something else he didn’t know before. Today might just have been his best idea ever.

Hollyn thanked Shawnee as Shawnee pulled the door closed, but not before winking once more at Noah. Could the woman be any more obvious?

“Forgot the movies, huh?” Hollyn said, smirking with a raised brow. She’d seen right through all that. Of course she did. They didn’t know the menial things about each other, but she knew him better than anyone ever had in his life.

Noah smacked her on the ass as she passed to pop the first movie in. “You want any junk food yet?” he asked.

“Ugh. No. I’m still too full,” she said.

She’d chosen *It* for their first movie. Noah sat on the couch, his arm thrown over the back cushions, his ankle crossed over his knee. Hollyn turned to sit on the couch and kind of froze, her eyes slowly moving over his body. And he felt that rush of heat she got when she was turned on.

“You are so gorgeous,” she breathed out. “I mean, who has arms that big?” she asked, kneeling on the couch and attempting to wrap both hands around one of his biceps. “They’re like freaking bowling balls.”

“You just have small hands,” Noah said and tried to ignore the blood rushing to his groin.

She released his arm and turned, plopping down on her butt with one of her legs tucked under her. The movie began to play and she snuggled into his side, her head on his chest, her arm wrapping around his middle. He took the opportunity and inhaled deeply. Her scent was addictive. So sweet and fresh. The frilly shit she used in the shower, the frilly shit she used in the laundry, and then there was her, that clean, fresh scent beneath it all. She’d switched shampoos since the last time she went shopping. This one smelled like apples.

“Are you sniffing my hair?” she asked, tilting her head back to look up at him.

"I like the way you smell," he admitted.

"Stop sniffing me and watch the movie, big boy."

He fucking loved when she called him that. It had started out almost sarcastic at first, but now it came out as more of a term of endearment.

Noah wrapped both arms around her and hugged her tight, pressing his lips to the top of her head. Damn, he loved this woman. He had no idea all those years what he'd been missing. He'd just figured he hadn't been built to be a mate since it hadn't happened yet. Hell, Colton was in his twenties and already found the woman of his dreams. Luke was still young enough it could happen for him. But Noah and Carter were older. Hell, Carter was already forty and Noah wasn't far behind.

If he'd known how good this shit could've been, he might just have been out actively searching for his mate, for Hollyn. That didn't make sense, though. How the hell could he search for someone he didn't even know existed? This love shit sure did mess with his thoughts.

Eventually, they were both engrossed in the movie. Hollyn would start a little in certain scenes and cuddle closer into his side. He loved the way she felt against him like that.

"Hey, Noah?" she said softly.

"Yeah?"

She pulled away just enough to look up at him. "How long have you owned Moe's?"

He had to think about that. How long had his parents been gone? "About twelve years. I inherited after my parents were killed in a car accident. My sister wanted nothing to do with it, so it became mine."

"I'm so sorry," she said, putting her fingertips to her lips. "They died in the same accident? You lost them both at the same time?"

"Yeah," he said, a little sadness hitting him with the memory of finding out he was orphaned. "It sucked. And I still miss them. But that's how they'd have wanted to go. I mean, not in a car accident, but together. They were crazy in love, even after thirty years of marriage."

"How old is your sister?"

"She's five years older than me. She lives in Illinois with her mate and cubs."

"You have nieces and nephews?"

"Nieces. Four of them. And they're spoiled rotten," he said, a wide grin accompanying the thought of those little girls. He hadn't seen them in almost a year and missed them like crazy. But both his and his sister's lives were busy and Katie knew Noah worked a crap ton since he'd take over dad's bar.

"Was your dad's name Moe?" Hollyn asked, laying her head in his lap and she looked up at him.

"Nope. Moe was his dog."

That had Hollyn sitting up. "Okay, I'm not sure which part to address first. Your dad named a bar after a dog and he owned a dog. I've never met a Shifter who had pets."

"Peyton has a cat, but she had him when she was still human. And that thing hates everyone but her. He barely tolerated Tristan."

Hollyn smiled at him with slightly wide eyes. "I wonder what would happen if we tried to get a dog," she said, her eyes moving to the side as if she were picturing it.

"Moe was an exception. Most animals can tell we're predators and stay away from us. But that dog was nuts. He tried to bite everyone, including my dad. When he'd had enough of it, he Shifted and roared at the dog. And Moe? Didn't run. Didn't whine. Didn't even cower. He just showed his teeth and growled. When Dad Shifted back to his human form, Moe approached him slowly, sniffing him all over. Then he licked his face. It was like Dad had to show the damn dog who was the Alpha. But that didn't stop him from snapping at anyone who tried to pet him. Dad took that dog to the bar every fucking day, even when he got warned for breaking the health code."

"I love when businesses have pets. It makes it feel so…I don't know, homey or something."

She took a piece of hair and twirled it around her finger. "We could try to get a dog. Or cat. Or something. I mean, I'm not a predator. Surely, a dog would love me."

"And piss all over the house when he felt threatened by me."

She tossed the hair back over her shoulder and narrowed his eyes at Noah. “Fine. But don’t be surprised if you come home some day and there’s a litter of puppies running around the house.”

Noah tried his hardest to appear stern and shook his head. But she just batted her lashes up at him and smiled sweetly. Fuck. He’d go adopt every dog from the kennel if it made her happy. But he had to at least appear to be putting up a fight.

The first movie ended and Hollyn stretched before standing to put the second in. This had been the longest he’d sat still in years and his ass was going to sleep.

“Let’s go outside for a while,” he said, needing some air and a little movement.

“Getting restless?” she asked, pushing the button to insert the disc but she didn’t hit play.

Noah walked out ahead of her, immediately lifting his head to scent the air. The more time passed with Aron unable to locate the jackoffs probably looking for Hollyn, the more anxious and overprotective Noah grew.

When he was sure they were alone, except his Clan who were all inside their own cabins, Noah moved so Hollyn could step out behind him. He took her hand and guided her toward the woods lining their property. She’d yet to roam their property with him. For some reason, her seeing all the property, her seeing where his bear ran, made their connection all that much more perfect.

“You want to Shift, don’t you?” she asked as they stepped past the tree line.

“I’m good,” he lied. He really, really wanted to Shift and walk with her as Bear. And Bear wanted to walk with her, too. But his animal was still too unpredictable when it came to their mate. And none of the others were around to step in if Bear got out of control. Nope. Strolling in his human form was just fine.

Her hand was so warm and small in his. The top of her head reached his shoulder. He’d known she was smaller but walking beside her like this reminded him of how fragile she really was. She didn’t have Shifter healing. She didn’t have claws and teeth to fight with. She had her magic, her fire, but how powerful was it? Could she defend herself or just fry one or two people? What if she was outnumbered? Then what?

"What's wrong?" Hollyn asked, glancing up at him as they walked. No doubt she felt the spike in his anxiety. But when she squeezed his hand, he realized he was crushing hers.

Easing up on the pressure, he looked down at her and slowed to a stop. "Just…everything," he admitted. "I hate not knowing where those fuckers are and if they're heading this way. I hate not knowing how the fuck Melinda found you. I hate not being able to be on the offensive when I don't even know what I'm trying to protect you from."

Hollyn raised her hand and cupped the side of his face. "Stop worrying about me all the time. We have no idea what tomorrow holds. Other than another long day at the bar," she said with a wink. "Let's just enjoy our day. 'Kay?"

Noah turned fully to face her. He wrapped one hand around the back of her neck and wrapped his arm around her waist, dragging her closer so he could taste her lips. He did promise her several orgasms and uninterrupted sexy time.

She tasted like heaven, just like she always did. Her hand spread on his chest and a hum of approval worked up her throat. He loved her sounds, loved to be able to pull those sounds from her. He loved that he could feel her arousal along with her emotions and loved that she reacted so strongly to his touch.

Hollyn broke the kiss the second he felt a spike in fear through their connection. Her eyes were wide and she looked around, looked in the direction they came, looked behind her.

"What's wrong?" he said, his body already beginning to tremble with his need to Shift to protect his mate.

"I feel her," Hollyn said, staying close to Noah as if she were trying to climb inside of him to hide.

"Melinda?" he asked, unable to suppress the deep growl that reverberated through his chest.

"Yeah," she said, a tiny tremble in her voice. "I feel her, but where the hell is she?" She was still looking around.

Noah lifted his face, like he had at the cabin, and tried to find her location. But he smelled nothing out of the ordinary. The constant breeze wasn't helping. She would be down wind and he wouldn't know it. Her scent would be blowing away from him.

For some reason, her fear wasn't affecting him as strongly as his own anger. One fucking day. That's all he'd wanted. He just wanted one day where he could spend some time with his mate. Why the hell couldn't that be possible?

"Why is she back?" Hollyn whispered as she continued to search for her.

"Your magic won't reach her?"

Hollyn shook her head. "She must be too far. Maybe she's not in the territory, just nearby. I don't know." She chewed on her bottom lip. "But why is she here."

Hollyn had told Melinda in no uncertain terms she wanted nothing to do with her. The woman obviously held a hatred for Shifters. He'd seen her plain as day in her eyes and the way she wrinkled her nose at Noah when she'd found out Hollyn and he were mated.

"Let's head back," Noah said, constantly scenting the air just in case Melinda decided to ambush Hollyn and try to beg her once again to follow her in her quest in finding more Fae.

Hollyn nodded, but her eyes were still on the trees around them, squinting as if that would help her see more clearly.

Carter and Luke were in front of Carter's cabin when Noah and Hollyn emerged. Luke's eyes were blazing bright amber, but it wasn't uncommon for him to be pissed. Ever since his perceived failure to protect Emory a couple of years ago, the dude had become a ticking time bomb.

The closer he got to his Clan brothers, the more uneasy she grew. It wasn't their glowing eyes or the fear rolling from Hollyn. It was something in the air, some kind of pressure that pressed down on his chest and made his heart beat a little faster. Or maybe that was Hollyn's heart.

Regardless, he sure as fuck didn't like it.

"You feel that?" Carter asked, his eyes doing like Hollyn's had in the woods and scanning the area. "What the fuck is that?"

"It's Melinda," Hollyn said, her voice more scared than she'd ever heard and it made his bear scratch at Noah's insides to be released. He wanted to kill whatever was scaring their mate.

"Where is she?" Luke growled. His teeth had Shifted and his words came out muffled from his mouth being overcrowded.

"I don't know. I can feel her, but I have no idea where she is and my magic can't reach her."

Noah guided Hollyn closer to Luke and Colton and let his bear have his body. There was no use fighting it. At least this way, the pain would reside quicker and his bear would be a lot less volatile if Noah didn't struggle to keep his skin.

Plus, Bear's sense of smell was a lot more acute than Noah's. He'd be able to pick something up that Noah might miss.

A series of pops sounded behind him, then Luke's massive bear was standing beside Noah. Their big bodies blocked any access to Hollyn, even if they didn't know who or what they were blocking. Even in his animal form, he couldn't pick up shit.

"Do you still feel her?" Carter asked as he rubbed a hand down his arm.

"Well, if you can, so can I," Hollyn said. She'd felt it in the woods before Noah had. Did that mean if they were feeling it, she had to be close.

"Are Fae able to cloak their presence?"

"What do you mean?" Hollyn asked, stepping closer to Bear until she laid a hand on his back.

"Can you mask your scent?" Carter asked.

"I'm not sure. If we can, I was never taught."

Of course, she wasn't. She hadn't had enough time with her parents to be taught all about her kind and her gifts.

Luke raised his snout into the air, then a deep, long growl rattled from his mouth as he bared his teeth in a snarl. Noah caught it about a half second later. He looked over his shoulder at Carter and tried to warn him they had incoming. And the scents weren't familiar.

****

Hollyn hid between Noah and Luke with Carter right behind her as she watched both bears lift their snouts in the air, then growl almost in unison. Did they smell Melinda? Why she was so scared after she'd already met the woman, she couldn't explain. There was just…something about the sensation in the air and rubbing against her skin.

Carter stepped around her and the bears and stood ahead of the three of them. She could see him tense as he watched in the direction where Noah and Hollyn had come from deep in the woods. Had someone been out there with them the whole time? How freaking creepy to think Melinda had been out there watching Noah and Hollyn make out when they'd had no idea she was there.

"What is it?" Hollyn whispered, terrified to raise her voice any louder.

"Shifters," Carter said, his voice a deep, growly sound, similar to how Noah sounded when he was fighting his animal.

Oh shit. Shifters. But she'd felt Melinda. Oh no! Did that mean they'd caught her? Were they just passing nearby, or were they coming to collect her, too? They'd make a killing from two female Fae.

Hollyn's hand tightened in Bear's fur and she stepped closer until she was wedged against his side. He glanced back at her and she watched his eyes bleed from his beast's amber to Noah's brown then back. They were both telling her they had her back, that they'd protect her, that they'd never let anything happen to her.

The pins and needles, staticky feeling grew until Hollyn wanted to rip her skin from her body. If the traffickers had caught Melinda, they had to help her. They couldn't allow them to see her off the way they were going to do to her. The way they'd done to thousands of other women.

"We can't let them leave with her," Hollyn said softly. Her throat was so tight she was surprised she'd gotten that much out.

Carter nodded once but didn't turn to face her. It was like he didn't want to turn his back on the woods, or whoever was in there.

Two more growls erupted from Luke and Noah's bears. Her hand tickled in Bear's fur from the vibration working through him. Noah turned just his body so that he blocked her from the woods, pinning her between the house and his big body. She had room to move, room to run inside if she needed, but there was no way anyone could sneak up behind her.

Her fight or flight instinct kicked in and she looked toward the trucks parked in the gravel. She could just jump in one of them and take off, go into hiding, blend in with humans in another town. But she'd have to leave Noah to do that. She was pretty sure she'd physically wither without her soul's other half.

She released her hold on Bear's fur and braced herself, putting her feet hip width apart. She wasn't sure how many were coming her way or what her warrior stance would even do to help her, but no way would she go down without a fight. She'd rather be dead than become someone's play toy, their sexual slave. Hell no.

Melinda appeared a few yards within the forest, her brows pulled together. Several men followed her. Three. Five. Eight. Shit. There were eleven men following Melinda. And she sure as shit didn't look like she was being restrained.

The wind picked up and whipped Hollyn's hair around her face. She tucked it behind her ears and glared at Melinda. She wasn't a prisoner; she was with them, showing them where Hollyn was. She might not have gotten a good look at the fuckers who'd poked her with that syringe, but her magic sure as hell recognized them.

"What the hell are you doing?" Hollyn asked, unable to even pretend to hide her rage at the fact Melinda was aiding a group of Shifters in kidnapping someone of her own kind. She knew damn well how endangered their species was. How could she be more motivated by money than her own people's survival?

"Just making a living," Melinda said with a smug smirk and a shrug. "You could still come on your own, you know. You could make this easier. Hell, you could even help me seek out more like you. Or, I could just make a lot of money. A pretty girl like you? With those boobs?" She nodded. "Oh yeah. The men would fork over the money in a heartbeat."

"You're trespassing on Blackwater territory," Carter said, trying his damnedest to avoid a fight.

Hollyn's phone was in he back pocket. She could pull it out and shoot a quick text or call Big River, ask for their help. No. She couldn't do that. She didn't want them involved.

As she thought about who else she could ask for a help, the sound of a vehicle bumping up the road met her ears a second after all the Shifters looked in that direction.

She recognized the car. She would've sagged with relief, but there were only two in that old Camaro. Brax parked the car and he and Daxon climbed, never even sparing her a glance. They kept their focus on the eleven assholes sneering and snarling at them. They must've recognized the panthers as the guys who'd gotten her away to begin with.

Brax pulled his shirt over his head as did Daxon. The tattoos across their chest, arms, and hands were stark, just black artwork across their tanned skin. Brax reached into his pocket and pulled out an elastic and wrapped it around his hair, keeping his chest length hair out of his face. If they Shifted to fight, he wouldn't have to worry; his beast had super short, coarse hair. Hollyn had felt it when she was learning to trust them.

Melinda turned just her eyes to the new arrivals and snorted softly with a roll of her eyes. "You really think they'll be of any help." She lifted her hands, palms up to indicate the eleven men behind and beside her. "Four against twelve."

"Six," Shawnee said as she and Colton stepped out onto the porch. "Six against twelve, bitch." Ooooh. Hollyn had never seen Shawnee angry before. But after learning what she'd went through with her family Pride, her anger was understandable. She was tired of people treating females as if they were livestock.

"You really think that ups your odds, little girl?"

Melinda was around Hollyn's height, maybe an inch shorter. Shawnee was only a couple of inches smaller. Maybe she was referring to Shawnee's young age. Either way, the condescending tone pissed Hollyn off. Her blood grew warmer as her ire spiked. Noah, or Bear, looked over his shoulder at her. He could feel it, he could feel her fire licking at her veins to punish something, or in this case, some*one*.

Turning his attention back to Melinda and her merry band of assholes, he showed his teeth and snarled.

"You can come willingly, or you can watch all your little friends die. Painfully, by the way," Melinda said.

Shawnee turned to Hollyn while Colton stepped ahead of her, his eyes on the threat. Her head shook side to side the slightest bit, but Hollyn had caught it. She was telling her to stay, not to give up, not to leave. She was telling Hollyn they were all prepared to fight for her. She was telling Hollyn they were all prepared to die for her. She was telling Hollyn they were a family and families stuck together until the end.

Melinda continued to smirk at Hollyn, but there was no way Hollyn would leave with this woman. For one thing, she was pretty sure Melinda was full of shit and she'd sell Hollyn off first chance she got. And for another…well, Melinda was full of shit. Even if Hollyn handed herself over, the Shifters who growled and snarled in their human forms would still attack the people she loved most.

"No deal," Hollyn said and smirked back at Melinda.

They might lose this fight. But Hollyn would die with her husband and her family.

The wind picked up and Hollyn's hair was in her face. She lost track of Melinda for a split second, but the bears and panthers didn't. As she pushed the hair away, pops echoed through the space and snarls assaulted her ears. Her entire Clan was now Shifted along with the panthers. They made a living wall in front of Hollyn, blocking Melinda and the now Shifted wolves from getting to her.

And then something clicked into place: the pins and needles sensation, the hair standing on end, the gusts of wind. Melinda was an Elemental Fairy, as well. Only she controlled energy. Shit. Hollyn could try to use her fire as a defense, but would the gusts of wind blow her flames out before they were of any use to her?

"Well? Get her so we can go,' Melinda yelled above all the noise coming from the huge beasts all around her.

Shit. Maybe she'd get lucky and Shawnee had texted Big River. Even if just the guys came to help, that would even out the odds and they'd have a fighting chance.

Even as she thought it, she hoped Shawnee didn't. It was bad enough her Clan was ready to fight by her side and possibly lose everything. She didn't need every single person she loved going down with them.

The wolves slowly advanced, snapping their teeth as if that would intimidate her people. But the bears and panthers, all but Noah, countered their move and kept them from coming too close. Noah stayed right there, his body almost pressed against hers. It felt like he was trying to back her up, back her closer to the house. But really, even if she hid inside, the wolves and Melinda could still get to her. It wasn't nothing more than wood and glass.

Melinda's eyes landed on Hollyn and a flash of evil glinted in her eye. For some reason, that look rubbed Hollyn in all the wrong ways. Fuck this bitch.

Raising her hand, Hollyn called forth her fire and more or less threatened to roast every single one of her buddies. Melinda just shook her head, never losing that stupid smirk. The wind picked up even more, but Hollyn's flame never died. It was part of her. She realized that now. Melinda couldn't blow it out anymore than she could blow Hollyn out.

But she learned quickly she could easily blow her over.

Melinda raised her hand, mimicking Hollyn, then thrust that hand toward Hollyn and Noah. Noah stumbled a few feet but Hollyn flew back, hitting the cabin hard. Her head throbbed and stars danced in her vision.

In a flash, it sounded like hell had broken loose. Hollyn shook her head and tried to focus on her surroundings. Three bears, a lion, and two panthers were fighting the wolves. Luke was having some success, slapping his gigantic paw at anyone who came near. Colton stayed close to Shawnee, keeping any of the wolves from jumping on her back. Carter charged at two wolves while Brax and Daxon were full on attacking two more. Even with her people fighting for her, wolves were making their way through them and to her.

Come on, she coaxed her flame, urging it higher, bigger, hotter. She'd never tried it, but if ever was the time it was now. Hollyn pulled her hand back and threw the ball of flame at two wolves who were advancing on Noah and Hollyn. Holy shit. It worked.

As quickly as she could, she conjured another ball of flames and threw it toward a wolf who was creeping up on Shawnee. That one didn't see it coming and got some singed fur. The smell wafted over to her on the nonstop wind coming from Melinda.

A freaking energy manipulator. That's why Hollyn had felt her so clearly, that's why she hadn't been able to find Melinda, and it had to be the way Melinda had found Hollyn. She'd followed her energy trail straight to Cedar Hill.

"What the hell is wrong with you?" Hollyn yelled at Melinda. "You sell off your own fucking kind. You're selling off women."

Melinda shrugged, lifted her chin, and a force of wind slammed Hollyn against the house to the point she could barely pull her head away from the side. Bear looked over his shoulder, growled deep and took a step toward Melinda. But when he did that, two wolves stepped to the side, just waiting for him to be clear of Hollyn.

Noah backed up until his rump was against Hollyn's legs. He nudged her but she was plastered against the rough wood.

"Your fire is nothing to me," Melinda said, barely raising her voice above conversational. It was hard to make out her words over the sounds of battle going on around her.

Luke was fighting two wolves while one clung to his back. Colton swatted a wolf off Shawnee's back while two clung to his and successfully knocked him off balance. Carter was struggling with three of his own. Two more wolves were still trying to get around Noah to Hollyn.

"This could've been you," Hollyn said, racking her brain for anything to buy her some time, distract Melinda enough to get free, anything.

Melinda actually narrowed her eyes and tilted her head. "What are you talking about now?"

"You could've been the one hunted. You're female, Fae, and have gifts. You could've been the one they hunted and sold off."

“I was, you stupid little twit,” Melinda said, dropping her hands and cutting the wind off. Hollyn dropped forward heavily, catching herself on Bear’s back.

Hollyn balled her hands into fists and called forward more fire balls, ready to chuck them at the first asshole who came close.

“I was hunted. I was captured. And I was sold. But unlike you, I cooperated. And my buyer came to like me. We became friends,” she said with a roll of her eyes. “Or he thought we did. I did everything I could to make that fucker fall in love with me. And then he had a little accident when we were on a cruise and a sharp breeze blew him over the side and straight into the Atlantic.”

“You killed him,” Hollyn said, inventorying her Clan from the corner of her eye, fearing if she gave Melinda even the smallest window she’d send her buddies forward.

“Of course I did. He deserved it. Trust me. Here’s the thing,” she said, leaning forward a little as if sharing a secret. “He had me on all his accounts. I didn’t even know until after he was dead. I just happened to return to the house, the bereaved lover, and rifled through his shit to make the past six years worth it. Yep. He’d made hundreds of thousands of dollars in trafficking. I just happened to keep him happy enough to avoid being sold off when he tired of me.”

Hollyn felt sick. Melinda had bent to that man’s desires. It had probably been all about survival at first. But the money, apparently, changed something inside her. Maybe she’d been broken during that time. Maybe she’d snapped under the pressure of being someone’s slave. So then, why the hell would she want to put another woman through it?

“When I realized how much money was in this line of business, I just couldn’t make myself walk away. It’s amazing the kind of loyalty you can buy,” Melinda said, tossing her hair over her shoulder.

Hollyn motioned to the fighting around her. “I didn’t have to buy their loyalty.”

Raising her hand, she grew the balls of fire as fast as she could and threw them directly at Melinda. The bitch successfully blew one away, but the other hit her legs, catching her pants on fire. She was too busy patting out the flame to notice another ball coming right for her fucking head.

How much more could she do? Could she make the flames higher? Hotter? The problem with her attack was she was too distracted to notice the wolves advancing. Bear turned in time to barrel into one of them, but the other one leapt right over his back.

Hollyn tossed flames at him as fast as she could, unable to check on Noah. Bear had to handle it, had to make sure both sides of her mate were safe. She had her own battle to worry about.

"Get that bitch! Kill the rest!" Melinda screamed. Hollyn could hear the rage in every word.

Kill the rest. Kill. Melinda wanted her family dead.

Hollyn threw another ball of flame at the wolf snapping his teeth at her and hit him on the nose. He yelped and jumped back, lowering his head and pawing at the burning fur and flesh on his muzzle. That gave Hollyn enough time to check on her family.

Her heart damn near stopped when she found each member of the Clan and the panthers. They were still fighting, but they were a bloody mess. No way would they win this if they kept going. The wolves barely had any wounds. They had plenty of energy and fight left in them.

She could surrender over to Melinda and pray she let them live. Or…

Hollyn sought out Bear, searched the thread for Noah buried deep inside of Bear's mind. She could feel his fear, his anger, his drive to keep going no matter what. But she felt his love the most. She felt how her mate, her husband felt about her. She held onto that and let Melinda's words bounce around in her head.

"You can't have them," Hollyn said as her hair continued to slap her in the face. She didn't even bother pushing it away anymore, just focused all her anger on Melinda. This bitch never knew her parents. In fact, she was old enough she very well could've been the one who led the attack on her family. She could've been there when her parents were murdered in cold blood.

Hollyn's veins were like molten lava and she could feel the tendrils of pain coming from Noah but he kept fighting. And so would she.

She would fight for her life. She would fight for her mate. She would fight for her family. And she would fucking win.

All the years of pent up anger came bursting free like a tidal wave. A wall of flame erupted toward the sky, reaching toward the top of the trees. Everyone stopped fighting almost immediately and stared. Noah backed toward Hollyn, even though she knew it had to hurt. While she was made up of these flames, they would burn Noah. They could kill him.

No. They couldn't. As sure as she knew they were no danger to her, her magic reassured her they were no danger to Noah. Her magic flowed through his veins now, too.

Hollyn made the wall of fire dance closer to Melinda. She backed closer to the tree line. Hollyn's family were on the move now, moving closer to Hollyn, staying away from the heat radiating from Hollyn's weapon.

"You could still come with me," Melinda said, her eyes wide as fear finally gripped her. "We could be partners. You could even check out the buyers before we send the women on."

Evil bitch. Even now, even when she realized there was no way she could win, she was thinking only about profits. And she thought Hollyn would want to be a part of something so disgusting?

The thing is, if Hollyn let this bitch leave, she'd just go on kidnapping women, taking them from their families and their lives, and selling them to be breeders, slaves, she didn't care. She didn't care if they were abused or passed around. All she cared about was making a buck.

Like something exploded from her chest, Hollyn gasped and threw her head back as another wave of flames erupted from her and slammed into Melinda. She screamed as she fell to the ground, fighting the flame.

A hand touched her forearm. She recoiled until her body recognized Noah before her eyes could focus. He'd Shifted back and was standing beside her completely naked. "Hollyn, don't. You'll never forgive yourself."

Forgive herself for what? For killing Melinda? For ending the suffering of dozens, maybe even thousands of women? But if Melinda died, the location of those women died with her. If Hollyn let her live, they could turn her over to the Shifter council and let them deal with her as if she were a Shifter. Their laws didn't pertain to Fae, but since they no longer had their own government, and since Melinda had been working with Shifters to sell off not only Fairy women but Shifter women, as well, she'd let the men and women of that government deal with her punishment. If Hollyn let her live, perhaps they could save all those women and deliver them back to their homes and families.

Force slammed back into Hollyn so hard it took her breath. Her flames retreated back into Hollyn so fast she felt like she'd burst into flames herself.

The wolves they'd been fighting looked at Hollyn with varying expressions, but they all held terror. There was no way they'd be able to hold these men for the Council. If they tried, it'd be another fight. She could always use her flame to keep them until someone came, keep them from fighting her family, but just because Noah was immune to the damage didn't mean the rest of them were.

The first wolf seemed to understand what was going on and backed away slowly, his head whipping back and forth between Hollyn and Melinda. When he hit the tree line, he turned and sprinted. Then, one by one, they all followed suit. Howls erupted deep in the forest until they faded to nothing.

Melinda was on the ground, lying in a fetal position. Smoke rose for her clothing and her skin was blistered.

"Someone call your people and have that bitch taken away," Hollyn said.

Everyone but Luke Shifted to their human forms. No. Luke continued to pace back and forth along the tree line. He was thinking about chasing after the men who'd helped Melinda steal females.

"It's too dangerous, Luke," Carter called out when he realized what Luke was doing.

Luke's bear looked over his shoulder at the stand-in Alpha and snarled.

Her people were still alive, still standing, but they'd been beat to shit. Only Hollyn was unscathed. They'd fought to keep the wolves away from her and had come so close to paying with their own lives.

Chapter Fourteen

Noah closed the bar on Monday. They were healing, but they were still all sore as hell. Hollyn had a feeling there would be more than one disgruntled customer when they returned to work. But she didn't care. And she knew he didn't. As he wrapped himself around her as if he were afraid she'd disappear the second he moved away, she knew the only thing that mattered to either of them were their family.

Big River had been pissed when they found out about the attack. Gray and Micah more or less went off on Carter for not calling them. But in the end, Hollyn was pretty sure they understood. They'd gone through enough and had children to worry about. Blackwater didn't want to endanger the pups or their parents.

Melinda had been taken into the Shifter Council by Nova's dad who was a member. He used to be higher up but chose to step down when Nova had come into his life. Since Melinda didn't have the same healing as the Shifters, she'd been seen by a Shifter doctor before being locked up. Noah had stopped Hollyn before she could do any permanent damage to the bitch, although she deserved it for what she'd done to all those women.

Hollyn hadn't slept much after the fight yesterday, but she couldn't make herself get out of the bed. She loved the weight of Noah's arm across her middle, the way his big body spooned up behind her, the way his muscular leg tangled with hers.

She could've lost him yesterday. She could've lost them all. And then there was the regret of losing her parents. Had she had the ability back then to stop what had happened to them? She knew she shouldn't dwell on it, that she was just a child, but it would always stay in the back of her mind.

Hollyn pulled Noah's arm tighter around her and thread her fingers through his. If it was up to her, they'd stay just like this for the rest of the week. Unfortunately, her body had other ideas. She had to use the bathroom and her stomach was growling.

“Wake up,” she whispered, turning just her head to try to look over her shoulder. Noah’s face was buried in her hair and pressed against the back of her neck, his breath warming the skin there.

He grunted but didn’t move.

“Your mate is hungry,” she said, hoping to appeal to his nurturing and protective nature.

That made him shift a little, but he just pulled Hollyn closer until the breath whooshed out of her. “Too tight,” she squeaked. She chuckled when Noah instantly reduced the pressure of his hold.

“Aren’t you hungry?” she asked, turning to face him now that he’d released his death grip on her.

“For you,” he grumbled, his eyes still closed.

“I’m starving.” She tried to slip out from under his arm, but he hooked his hand around her hip and dragged her back. He nuzzled his face against her neck again, his thick beard scratching and tickling her.

Hollyn squealed and giggled. Unfortunately, that encouraged him and he attacked her ribs with his fingers. When she was able to get out from under him and off the bed, the air left her lungs in a rush. He was so battered and scarred. There were fading bruises on his face, his arms, his chest. Silvery pink scars criss crossed almost every inch of his flesh from his neck down. He’d taken that beating to protect her.

“Do they hurt?” she asked, kneeling and running a finger along one of the puckered lines.

Noah’s eyes opened and he tucked his chin to watch her stroking the scar that would be nothing more than faint lines by tomorrow.

“Not really.”

“You could’ve died,” she breathed out, her eyes watering and blurring her vision.

“You wouldn’t have let that happen.” His voice was strong and confident, and a little scratchy with sleep. He rubbed the heel of his hands against his eyes and pushed up to lean against the headboard with a grunt and a groan. “You were amazing. My little bad ass,” he said with a slow smile.

“If I’d figured it out earlier, I could’ve avoided all of you getting injured.”

"If you'd never done it before, how the hell do you think you could've figured it out earlier. We heal fast, Hollyn. This is nothing," he said, waving his hand down his body. "Should've seen us after Shawnee's family Pride attacked."

"I don't want to think about that. And I never want to see you like this again," she said, angrily swiping the tear that rolled down her face away with her fingertips.

Noah gently wrapped his fingers around her biceps and pulled her closer. When she was close enough, on her and knees, he cupped the back of her head and pressed a kiss to her lips. It wasn't sexual. It was comforting. It was possessive. It was a reassurance that everything was fine now, they were safe and together.

He pulled away but stayed close enough his face was out of focus. "I love you so much," he said.

As if a switch was flipped, all that fear and anger fled and was replaced by the warmth coming from Noah, the love he felt squeezing her heart.

"I love you more," she said, sounding like Shawnee the first day they'd all met.

Pounding on their front door echoed through the house. Hollyn tensed, but Noah just growled and shook his head. Throwing the blankets off, he moved toward the bedroom door and threw it open hard enough for it to hit the wall and bounce off.

"What are you doing? Who is it?" Hollyn asked, jumping to her feet and yanking on her clothes.

Noah didn't seem even a tiny bit nervous, which meant either he could hear whoever it was or scented them.

"Reed," he said and stepped into the hallway.

"Wait! You're naked," Hollyn called, running after him as he pulled her shorts over her butt.

The fact he was about to answer the door with his junk flopping in the wind didn't seem to phase him. He just yanked the door open and glared at Reed.

Reed instantly threw a hand up to block the view. "Dude! Put on some pants."

"What do you want?" Noah grumbled in that gruff tone he used with everyone but Hollyn.

"Here," he said, thrusting a rather tall pile of DVDs at Noah while still keeping his eyes averted.

Noah continued to glare at Reed with his arms crossed over his chest. Hollyn knew her man was big, but seeing him standing in the doorway, his head barely a couple inches from the top of the frame, she finally realized she'd married a freaking giant.

"Thanks, Reed," Hollyn said, taking the movies from him.

"I heard you didn't have any movies. Shawnee said she had to loan you a few. I wasn't sure what you were into, so I brought over a few different genres."

Lola had told Hollyn all about her mate's obsession with movies and that he'd named their daughter Grace after Grace Kelly. This was a moment Hollyn was grateful for his obsession.

"Oh! I haven't seen that one," Hollyn said as she skimmed over the titles.

Reed turned to say something, then turned his face to the side when he remembered Noah was naked. The Shifters were always naked around each other when they Shifted, but maybe it was the way Noah was glaring at him while buck naked that was making Reed so uncomfortable.

"If there's anything else you're in the mood for or a movie you've been wanting to see, just let me know. I'm sure I have it."

"How do you have room for all those movies when you have a baby?"

Reed shrugged. "I rented a storage unit in town." He said it as if it should be obvious and made Hollyn laugh. Reed looked at her this time, completely ignoring Noah. "I heard what happened. What you did. Thank you for protecting everyone. But next time, give us a call. You know we would've been here in a heartbeat to help you guys. They've helped us plenty of times," he said, jerking his chin toward Noah.

That seemed to soften Noah a little and he dropped his arms and cupped himself in both hands. 'Cause yeah, it took both hands to hide his man meat.

"I've got to get back. Lola and I are actually going on a date tonight, without all of Big River," Reed said, his brows high as he smiled.

"Have fun," Hollyn said.

Reed hesitated on the porch for another minute. He looked like he wanted to ask something or say something. But he just stepped forward and hugged Hollyn around the shoulders, earning a growl from Noah. He stepped back and Hollyn could've sworn his eyes looked a little misty.

"Seriously, though. Thank you. And I'm glad you're okay. And still here. You're part of this screwed up gang now," Reed said. His grin got comically big and he practically bounced down the stairs and climbed into his truck. He put his hand out the window for one last wave as he bumped along the gravel drive and disappeared around the corner.

"He's a weirdo, but he means well," Noah grumbled, pulling Hollyn into the house so he could close the door.

"I can't believe you answered the door naked. What if Lola had been out there with him?" she asked, plopping onto the couch and flipping through the foot tall stack of movies.

"I would've heard or scented her," he said, confirming her earlier question.

Noah sat next to her and she suddenly had a hard time focusing on the DVDs. A naked Noah was something she would never be able to ignore. Hollyn leaned back, lifted his arm, and ducked underneath, resting her cheek on his chest and listening to his heart thump to the same beat as hers. She spread her fingers on his chest. Closing her eyes, she sighed with contentment. They'd made it. And maybe now that the jackasses who'd helped Melinda realized she wasn't an easy target and had people who loved her and would fight for her, she might just be able to live her life without constantly looking over her shoulder.

And then maybe…

"What are you thinking about?" Noah asked. There was a smile in his voice.

"Why do you ask?" she replied without opening her eyes. She was just fine snuggled into his side and would prefer to stay right there for the rest of the day. Or at least until she could no longer ignore the hunger pangs.

"Because I just got a wave of excitement and your heart is beating a little faster," he said, wrapping his arms around her and kissing the top of her head.

Hollyn pulled back and smiled when Noah pouted at the loss of her in his arms. "You're going to think I'm crazy," she said and wondered if her cheeks were pink.

His eyes bounced all over her face. "Tell me."

She sucked her lips into her mouth and dropped her eyes as she wondered how he'd feel about what she had to say. "I was just thinking…since we know I'm not exactly a damsel in distress and have these super hero powers, and Melinda is no longer a threat, and those assholes probably aren't stupid enough to come back…" She trailed off, the rest of the words stuck in her throat.

His eyes narrowed. "What?"

She picked up his big hand and played with his fingers. "I was just thinking…maybe it'll be safe for us to have a family together."

When Hollyn finally raised her eyes to his face, she almost melted. Noah's eyes held the tiniest glow and they glistened.

"A family. Kids," he said, his voice thick. She nodded. "You want to have babies with me? Even if we don't know if they'll be a bear or a Fairy or a mixture of the two?" She nodded again.

Noah grabbed her roughly and pulled her forward. She hit the warmth of his chest the same time his lips crashed down on hers.

He didn't part his lips, didn't touch hers with his tongue, just kept his lips smashed against hers, holding her so tight she once again had to push him away for a little air.

He released her just enough for her to look in his eyes, but kept his arms wrapped around her.

"I take that as a yes? You want to try for children with me?"

Noah stood and scooped her in his arms so fast she squealed and jogged toward the bedroom. "Hell yes," he said as he dropped her onto the bed and began to peel her clothes from her.

She'd meant eventually, but who was she to stop her mate if he wanted to make love to her.

####

If you enjoyed Noah's Fire, Lynn would be over the moon if you left a review on Amazon and/or Goodreads. You can also find her on Facebook here.

About the Author

Lynn Howard lives in Cedar Hill, MO, where all her sexy Shifters exist. She lives and breathes hot Alpha males and sassy brassy females. She feels the most at home knee deep in mud and chicken muck and prefers to be outside under the stars, cuddled up under a blanket in front of a bonfire than in the big city.

When not typing away or feeding her chickens, you can find her fantasizing about hot country boys for her next book or wandering the woods in search of wildlife. She loves all animals and insects...except spiders. Her favorite foot accessory is barefoot and she owns at least twenty sets of salt-n-pepper shakers, yet only uses one.

Gray's Wolf is the first in the Big River Pack series. And just like in Gray's Wolf, there are more hot country boy Shifters just waiting to their turn for a little love and romance.

Reading Order

Big River Pack:

Gray's Wolf

Micah's Match

Emory's Mate

Reed's Girl

Tristan's Voice

Blackwater Bears:

Colton's Kitty

Noah's Fire

Character Index

Big River Pack

Grayson (Gray) Harvey – Alpha – wolf
Micah Matthews– Second – wolf/coyote hybrid
Reed Peterson – wolf
Tristan – wolf
Peyton Mathes – wolf – mate to Tristan
Nova Harvey – wolf – mate to Gray
Callie Taylor – mate to Micah
Lola Braun – wolf – Reed's mate

Blackwater Clan

Carter – bear
Colton Barnes – bear
Luke – bear
Noah – bear – owner of Moe's Tavern
Shawnee Baker aka Fancy Pants – lioness – mate to Colton

Ravenwood Pride

Aron – Alpha – panther
Mason – panther
Brax – panther – brother to Daxon
Daxon – panther – brother to Brax

Deathport Pack

~~Anson – Alpha – wolf~~
Felix – Second – wolf
Barrett – wolf
Kaleb – wolf
Tanner – wolf

Tammen Pride

~~Rhett – Alpha – lion~~
Trever – lion
~~Brent – lion~~
Brian – lion
Chuck – lion – owner of Dodson's Garage

Council Members

Alan Price – wolf - Nova's biological dad
~~Frank – wolf – Colton's dad~~

<u>Hope Pride</u>
Eli – lion - Alpha
Emory – wolf – Eli's mate
Luna – lioness – sister to Eli
Amber – lioness
Petra – lioness

<u>Remsen Pride</u>
~~Jace – lion – Emory's former mate~~

<u>Morse Pack</u>
Eric Branes – wolf – Second
Koda – Alpha
Carl Braun – wolf – Lola's dad

Made in the USA
Middletown, DE
11 May 2021

39487062R00113